Please return/renew this item by the last date shown.
Library items may also be renewed by phone on
030 33 33 1234 (24hours) or via our website

www.cumbria.gov.uk/libraries

Cumbria Libraries

CLIC
Interactive Catalogue

Ask for a CLIC password

LINWOOD BARCLAY

ESCAPE

Orion
Children's Books

ORION CHILDREN'S BOOKS
First published in Great Britain in 2018
by Hodder and Stoughton

1 3 5 7 9 10 8 6 4 2

Text © NJSB Entertainment Inc. 2018

The moral rights of the author have been asserted.

A CIP catalogue record for this book is available from the British Library.

ISBN 978 1 5101 0221 7

Typeset by Hewer Text UK Ltd, Edinburgh
Printed and bound in Great Britain by CPI Group (UK) Ltd, Croydon CR0 4YY

The paper and board used in this book are from well-
managed forests and other responsible sources.

Orion Children's Books
An imprint of
Hachette Children's Group
Part of Hodder and Stoughton
Carmelite House
50 Victoria Embankment
London EC4Y 0DZ

An Hachette UK Company

www.hachette.co.uk
www.hachettechildrens.co.uk

For Neetha

01

The van was flying.

Jeff Conroy stared out the window, nose to the glass, breathless. Seconds earlier, they'd been driving along on solid ground, but now their rusty old van was sailing through the sky.

The road was so far below that it looked like a snake winding its way through the grass. Except those weren't blades of grass. They were trees. And those weren't little model houses or toy cars like you'd find on a train set. They were the real thing.

As amazing as it might seem to be in a van that could fly, Jeff was not enjoying the ride. He was scared, and feeling more than a little sick to his stomach as the vehicle swayed back and forth through the air.

The van continued to sail along gracefully, but the view out the windows was partially obscured by the thick black magnetic straps that clung to the van's metal body. They led up to the large helicopter above, and had been used to lift the vehicle off the road.

Harry Green, sitting at the now totally useless steering wheel, glanced back helplessly at Jeff, who was in the middle of the van, next to his dog Chipper.

"What are we going to do, Chipper?" Jeff shouted over the noise of the rotating chopper blades as he looked at the ground far below.

Chipper did not know. Chipper had only just woken up.

* * *

Five minutes ago, before their van had been tracked down by The Institute, Chipper had been dreaming.

Even though there were almost no other dogs like Chipper on the entire planet, he still resembled the most common of mutts in at least one respect.

When he slept, he dreamt.

While the scientists at The Institute had spent millions of dollars to create what was in effect a running, barking, sniffing computer, outfitted with some of the most sophisticated software ever invented, the one thing they could not do was keep it awake twenty-four hours a day.

Chipper could read multiple languages, access maps in his head and do complicated calculations but, unlike an ordinary laptop that could run all the time, Chipper sometimes needed to lie down, shut his eyes and catch a few winks. Well, he didn't have to shut his eyes, considering they weren't real ones, but he could put them into sleep mode.

And when Chipper did finally drift off, he had dreams. Sometimes they were happy dreams, and sometimes they were nightmares.

Before the van became airborne, Chipper had been having a very happy dream, a dream of happier times.

He was dreaming about when he was a puppy.

Oh, what a glorious time it was, before his body was outfitted with chips and wires and circuitry and memory banks. Back then, Chipper's thoughts weren't like the ones he had now. These days, Chipper tended to think in actual words, just like people, but when he was a puppy it wasn't like that at all. There were impulses, and instincts, and feelings of joy and fear and curiosity.

There was so much to be curious about. He'd been born on a farm, one of a litter of four. Two brothers and one sister. The people who owned the farm had given them all names. He was Chipper, of course, and his sister was Bonnie, and his brothers were Scout and Wonder. Their mother, a beautiful border collie, was called Princess.

If you were a dog, a farm was the best place in the world to be born and raised. So many smells! Hay and grasses and trees and cows and chickens and millions

3

of scents! For a dog, whose nose was sensitive to smells, it was overwhelming, but in a good way. And unlike those poor, sad city dogs, who had to sit around all day in houses or apartments waiting for their owners to come home, and who might only get a few minutes each day to sniff about outside in the real world, all the while leashed to someone trailing along after them carrying a little plastic clean-up bag, farm dogs had it made.

You could run and run and run all day long. You could –

"Chipper!"

– round up the sheep or chase squirrels or hang out watching the cows get milked or jump into the back of your owner's pickup truck and be driven all over the property. You could flop down on your side in the dirt, in the sun, and feel the heat through your fur.

These were Chipper's memories when he had a dream. In many of them, he was with his mom.

In the dreams, Chipper had the power of speech. He could tell his mother how much he loved her. He could tell her how much he liked life on the farm, and how he would never, ever leave.

But then, sometimes, the dreams would turn dark, as dark as the SUV that arrived one day. The SUV with the men in dark suits, the men from The Institute.

Chipper would plead with his mother not to make him go away with the men. He wanted to be a regular dog for ever. He –

"*Chipper!*"

He didn't want anyone opening him up and putting in all sorts of fancy equipment. He didn't want anyone taking away his real eyes and replacing them with cameras so that the people back at The Institute could see what he saw. He didn't want anyone giving him the ability to figure out what seven times fifteen times eleven divided by sixteen was.

Who needed to know that when you were a dog?

Sometimes, when he was having a dream like this, Chipper tried to make the men get back into their black SUV, turn around and leave the farm. Sometimes he was able to do it, and sometimes he wasn't. This was turning into one of those times when –

"*Chipper!*"

Chipper activated his eyes.

Where was he? And who was this boy yelling at him?

Oh, right. He was in an old Volkswagen camper van. Harry Green, that guy in his late sixties who'd been staying in one of the cabins at the boy's fishing camp, was up front behind the steering wheel. And the boy in the back, sitting right next to Chipper, waking him up, was Jeff, his twelve-year-old friend, the one he had set out to find when he'd busted out of The Institute.

"Were you dreaming?" Jeff asked. "I couldn't wake you up!"

Jeff was holding a cell phone in his hand, the kind that could do everything from make phone calls to surf the Internet. But the only thing Jeff used it for now was texting. And not even to write texts, but to receive them.

From Chipper.

As advanced as Chipper was, he could not actually speak. He could think things. And those thoughts could be translated into words that were then transmitted as texts to Jeff's phone. Jeff's friend Emily had figured it out. She was one smart cookie.

Jeff didn't have to text to Chipper. All he had to do was talk to him and Chipper understood every word.

Chipper responded.

Yes. I was dreaming.

Jeff glanced at the phone and read the response. Chipper noticed that the boy looked very anxious. Chipper also quickly became aware the van was driving very quickly. He hopped up on the seat at the tiny dining table. The battered old van also had a bed at the back with storage underneath, a tiny stove and refrigerator, and a narrow closet to hold odds and ends.

They were on a country lane. A quick glance ahead and back revealed that the van was the only vehicle on the road. But Chipper was hearing more than just the van's rasping engine. There was something above them.

What is happening?

"They've found us."

Chipper did not have to ask who had found them. That would be The Institute. But as far as Chipper could tell, they were not being followed.

Where are they?

Jeff's index finger pointed straight up.

Chipper stuck his head out an already open window. His black and white fur fluttered in the high wind as he craned his neck to look up.

They were being chased by a helicopter.

"Does he see it?" Harry shouted.

He had helped Jeff and Chipper get away from the fishing camp Jeff's aunt ran after The Institute had tracked them down there.

"He sees it," Jeff said.

"He got any bright ideas?"

"You got any ideas, Chipper?" Jeff asked.

Chipper thought. He did not have any, at least not yet.

Working on it.

As he transmitted those words to Jeff's phone, thick black straps dropped from the sky alongside the van.

They reminded Jeff of the brushes in a car wash. Back when he still lived with his parents, when they

7

were still alive, they used to take their car through the wash, and Jeff had loved to watch the brushes slapping and dragging along the vehicle.

But these were different. They dangled and fluttered in the air like huge strands of dark fettuccine and then, suddenly, latched on to the car, as though they were magnetic. Five straps down the right side of the van, five straps down the left.

"What the heck is that?" Harry shouted.

He turned the wheel hard one way and then the other, swerving down the highway at more than seventy miles per hour. Veering left, then right, trying to shake those bands off the van.

I think we are in trouble.

"What's he saying?" Harry shouted.

"He thinks we're in trouble!" Jeff replied.

"Oh, well, thanks for that, Lassie!"

Harry continued to yank back and forth on the wheel, sending the van swerving all over the road.

But suddenly, when Harry turned the wheel, there was no response. The van did not do what it told him to do.

"What the—" Harry said.

The black bands on the side of the vehicle went rigid. Jeff peered out the window, down at the road. Chipper did the same from the other side of the van.

"Oh no," Jeff said.

Yeah. Oh no.

8

That was when the van began to lift off the road and fly over the countryside.

Which soon led to Jeff's big question: "What are we going to do, Chipper?"

Chipper wished he had a good answer to that.

FOUR DAYS EARLIER

They had been driving for hours. Jeff had no idea where they were. Harry Green said that was the best way to do things. Keep moving.

"We'll find a different place to stay every night," he'd told Jeff and Chipper after they had driven away from Flo's Cabins, the fishing camp on Pickerel Lake where Jeff had been living with his aunt, Florence Beaumont.

They'd had to flee after being tracked down by a team of agents from The Institute. The most dangerous one was a guy named Daggert. He'd captured Jeff and Chipper and had been taking them away in a boat when Jeff's friend, Emily Winslow, had saved them. Daggert's boat had blown up, but Jeff hadn't taken much comfort from that. The Institute would not rest until they had recovered the dog.

Chipper was a technological marvel and The Institute simply could not allow another organisation or government to get their hands on him. They would rather destroy him than allow someone else to acquire him.

So Harry had volunteered to hide Jeff and the dog until they could come up with a plan. After a few hours on the road, Harry, using a screwdriver from the glove compartment, had removed the licence plates from the van and swapped them with a set on a car he found parked behind a restaurant.

"There's cameras all over," he said to Jeff, who was sitting up front next to him. "Don't want them spotting our plate. And just to be sure, we stay off the interstate highways and toll roads. And we won't follow any predictable route. We'll head east one day, south the next, west the next. That way, if someone's trying to track us, if they pick up the scent, they won't say, 'Oh, hey, they're heading that way. We'll be waiting for them.' Nope, not gonna happen."

"What do you think?" Jeff asked Chipper, whose head was between them. The dog had his front paws on the centre console, his hind legs on the floor of the back seat. Perched that way, he could see out the front windshield.

A single word came up on Jeff's phone.

Maybe.

All other functions on Jeff's phone had been deactivated so that it could not be traced. It could not make calls or connect to the Internet. All it did now was act as a device to communicate with Chipper, and he could thank Emily for figuring out how to set that up.

"What do you mean?" Jeff said.

We cannot keep doing this for ever.

"What's he say?" Harry asked.

Jeff told him.

"I'm not saying for ever," said Harry. "Just until we figure things out."

"Why are you doing this?" Jeff asked. "Why are you helping us?"

Harry glanced over. He looked surprised by the question. "Are you kidding? Why wouldn't I?"

"You hardly know me," Jeff said. "You're just some guy who was renting a cabin from my aunt. You were having a nice summer, going fishing every day. Why put all that aside and run the risk of getting yourself killed to help some kid and his dog?"

Harry shrugged. "Well, first of all, that is not some ordinary dog you got there. Second, I'm retired and don't exactly have any other commitments. And third," and he looked at Jeff, "maybe I just cared. I saw a boy in trouble and I didn't see how I could turn my back on him."

Jeff said, "I'm sorry."

"No, don't be sorry."

"No, I feel bad. You're helping me and I'm not acting very grateful. My mom used to say I didn't always appreciate the things other people did for me."

15

"I'm sure she wasn't mad at you," Harry said. "It's just, sometimes, when you're a kid, you're not aware how much your mom and dad do for you. That's all. I bet, after she got mad, she did something nice for you."

Jeff felt his eyes moisten. "She would take me out for an ice cream," he said, remembering.

"There, you see."

Chipper leaned Jeff's way and licked his cheek. Jeff put his arm around the dog's head and gave him a gentle squeeze.

"I think my mom and dad would have liked you," Jeff told Harry.

"And I bet I would have liked them," he said. "You know what I'm gonna have to do? I'm gonna have to get us some cash. We're not going to put a lot of stuff on charge cards and have them figure out where we might be. We're coming up on a little town, oughta be able to get some here."

Jeff said, "Where from?"

"A cash machine, where else? There might be a bank, or maybe a convenience store. A lot of them have cash machines."

That might not be a good idea.

Jeff said cautiously, "Harry, I don't know a lot about these things, but if you use a machine, can't they track you just like they would if you used your credit card?"

"Huh?"

"If you use your bank card, and take out money, they'll know. The Institute is probably watching for something like that. And I think a lot of those machines, they have cameras that take pictures of everybody who uses them."

Harry said, "Oh, yeah, well, don't worry about that. I got that covered."

Chipper and Jeff exchanged looks. What was Harry talking about?

The van slowed as they entered the small town.

"Bunch of stores and things up ahead," Harry said. "Keep your eyes peeled for a bank."

"Uh, there's one," Jeff said, pointing. "At that first corner."

"Right you are." Harry steered the van over to the kerb and found a parking spot. "Chipper, look behind the rear seat, you'll see a green backpack. Can you grab that for me?"

Chipper leapt through to the back of the van, found the backpack, grabbed the strap between his teeth and worked his way back to the front of the van.

"Great, thanks," Harry said, taking the bag from the dog. He unzipped the bag, dug in, and pulled out what looked like small clumps of hair.

Jeff said, "Harry, what—"

"Hang on," Harry replied, adjusting the rear-view mirror so he could see his face in it. He began carefully

17

applying the hair to his face. A moustache first, then a beard.

He looked at Jeff and grinned. "What do you think?"

"Harry, why do you keep a disguise in your backpack?" Jeff asked. And then it hit him. "Harry, you're not going to *rob* the bank, are you?"

"What?" Harry said, smoothing down the beard, then going back into the bag and pulling out a wig.

"Is that what you are? A retired bank robber?"

Harry slipped the wig over his head. He'd been nearly bald to begin with, but now he had straggly grey hair.

That looks pretty good.

"I am not a bank robber," he said. "I used to be part of an amateur theatre group and we had to wear all kinds of different costumes and things."

"But why do you have all this stuff in your van?" Jeff wanted to know.

Harry found a Blue Jays baseball cap in the bag and put it on. "Well, almost everything I *have* is in the van. When I took that cabin for the summer at your aunt's place, I thought, hey, what if there's a local theatre troupe? Right? I'd be all ready to go."

Jeff gave Harry a disbelieving look.

"That's the story, whether you like it or not," Harry said. "Be back in a jiff."

He got out of the van. Jeff and Chipper watched him walk down the sidewalk and turn into the bank.

18

"Does that seem a bit fishy to you?" Jeff asked Chipper.

What is amateur theatre?

Clearly, there were some gaps in Chipper's knowledge, Jeff thought. "Acting. Putting on a play. You know what I mean by that?"

Yes.

"Do you think there's anything funny about Harry?"

Chipper thought before transmitting a reply.

Funny ha ha?

"No, funny, like, is there something he's not telling us about himself?"

Before Chipper could offer an opinion, Harry was coming out of the bank and heading straight for the van.

When he got back in, he waved a thin wad of cash before Jeff and Chipper.

"Five hundred bucks," he said. "That should keep us going for a while. Who feels like some lunch? I'm buyin'."

03

Madam Director had deliberately kept Daggert, The Institute's head of security, waiting. She was eager to know what progress he was making, but she also wanted to torture him a little, so she made him wait in her outer office for nearly thirty minutes. Finally, she tapped a button on her desk and said, "Send him in."

The door slid open and Daggert entered. He was wearing his usual black suit, white shirt and black tie. He had tucked a pair of sunglasses into the breast pocket of his jacket.

Madam Director did not rise from behind her desk, nor did she invite Daggert to take a seat. He stood at attention, hands locked behind his back.

"Daggert," she said, taking off her own oversized glasses to view him. She brushed a lock of her long red hair from in front of her eyes.

"Yes, Madam Director."

"Must be nice to be in some dry clothes.

I understand you had something of a boating mishap yesterday."

"Yes." He cleared his throat.

"So tell me, how old is this Emily Winslow girl, the one that outsmarted you, the one who got the boy and the dog away from you?"

"Thirteen," Daggert said. "She clearly knew that lake better than we did. She led us on to a rock ledge just below the surface—"

"Excuses, Daggert? Excuses from a man who's been here eight years, who once worked for the CIA and Special Forces?"

"I was only explaining—"

"How you were made a fool of by a child?"

Daggert said nothing.

"What are we doing about her?"

"Nothing, at least not now. Her father is a former police officer. We're treading carefully. But we're monitoring their calls. Emails, everything. They don't know where the boy and the dog are. We're watching places where we think the boy might turn up."

"Tell me more about him," Madam Director said. "It was no coincidence, was it? The dog was looking for that specific young man."

"Yes. The boy is Jeff Conroy. His parents were Edwin and Patricia Conroy."

"Who worked for us."

"Yes."

"Before perishing in that dreadful plane accident."

"Yes."

"Which was not an accident."

Daggert's chest puffed out ever so slightly. "Correct. They didn't like the direction The Institute's work was headed. There was reason to believe they might disclose information, go to the press."

"Yes, yes," Madam Director said. "That much I know. What about the Conroys and subject H-1094?"

Chipper's file number.

"They worked with that particular animal extensively," Daggert said.

Madam Director nodded. The Conroys had been very valuable members of the team. From the beginning, they'd been working on the hybrid dogs – part canine, part computer – that could be sent into hostile environments to record and gather information. A human spy going around asking questions attracted unwanted attention. But who paid attention to a dog? A dog could insinuate itself into places no person could.

The trouble with Chipper was that his natural instincts ran contrary to the goals of the mission. The dog could be in the middle of tailing a potential terrorist, see a squirrel, and go running off in the opposite direction to catch it. Which was why The Institute had decided Chipper had to be deactivated, put down. But Madam Director's staff had been outwitted and the dog had escaped.

So, the Conroys had worked with this dog, and when it got free of The Institute, it immediately went looking for their son.

Why?

Madam Director posed the question to Daggert.

"I have a theory," he said.

"I would love to hear it," she responded.

"They must have spoken of the boy when they were modifying H-1094. When the animal escaped, it remembered. It may have thought the Conroy boy would look after it, that he would provide a safe home for it. It may also have felt a need to protect the boy, knowing that his parents were dead."

"Maybe," Madam Director said. "And what do we know about this Harry Green person?" she asked.

"A retired fisherman, staying at Flo's Cabins," Daggert said.

"What's his background? Who is he?"

Daggert hesitated. "Well, the thing is, Harry Green is a very common name. There are thousands of them."

"Go on."

"And we're checking up on the ones that fit his profile, but . . ."

"But what?"

"We can't seem to find anything on this specific Harry Green," Daggert said. "It's like he never existed."

Madam Director gave Daggert a stern look. "How long had he been renting that cabin?"

"All this summer," Daggert said.

"What about other summers?"

"So far as we know, this was his first year. And there's some info coming in that he may have been living in the nearby town, alone, before renting the cabin."

"So his arrival coincides, roughly, with the boy's."

Daggert nodded slowly.

"Like he was waiting, in case the dog ever escaped, for it to show up. Because he knew it would seek out the boy." She paused. "How many foreign governments and rival agencies do you think would like to get hold of one of our animals?" she asked him.

"The list would be long," Daggert said.

"Yes. Yes, it would. I wonder which one this Harry Green might be working for."

"And there's no chance he's actually working for us?" Daggert asked. "It's not unheard of for some agencies to pit their own people against each other to achieve their goals."

Madam Director smiled. "I'm flattered you think I could be that devious." She tapped her fingernails on the desk. "I have an idea."

"Yes?"

"Suppose local law enforcement were informed that a boy and his dog have been abducted by a man who looks like this Harry Green? And, if spotted, they should be reported to one of our cover agencies?"

Daggert nodded slowly. "More eyes on the lookout. It's a good idea."

"Of course it is," Madam Director said. "It was mine."

04

"How long will you be gone?" Jeff asked his mother.

He was standing in the doorway to his parents' bedroom, watching his mom pack a small carry-on suitcase.

"Just two nights," Patricia said, folding a blouse and tucking it into the side of the case. "You'll have fun, staying with your friend."

"And what about Pepper?"

As Jeff said her name, his dog Pepper padded into the bedroom. She rested her head on the bed and watched Patricia.

"She's going with you. The Thomases are happy to take you and Pepper. They love dogs. Kevin likes Pepper, doesn't he?"

Jeff nodded sullenly. He didn't like it when his parents went away.

"Why are you going?" he asked.

"It's a meeting," she told him. "The drug companies have lots of meetings to talk about all the new medicines they're coming up with."

"So people can have longer lives?" he asked.

"Not just longer, but better ones."

"If no one ever got sick, and no one ever died, the Earth would overflow with people," Jeff said.

Patricia stopped packing, looked at her son and smiled. "I guess, eventually, everyone will die of something. But while we are alive, we want to be as healthy as possible, to make the most of the time we have."

"I guess," Jeff said, not entirely convinced. "But what if—"

"Patsy!"

Jeff's father came into the room, looking harried. He ruffled the top of his son's head.

"The taxi's here," he said. "Aren't you packed yet?"

"I'm ready, Edwin. I was just tossing in some last things."

"Well, zip up that bag, or we're going to miss our flight."

Moments later, Jeff took Pepper across the street to his friend Kevin's house. Before going in, he stood and watched his parents' taxi drive down the street until it reached the corner, and turned out of sight.

* * *

Sitting in the back of the taxi, Patricia reached over and clutched her husband's hand.

"I'm scared," she whispered.

"I know," he replied. "Me too."

"What if something happens to us? What if they—"

"Nothing will happen to us," Edwin said. "Once we tell the newspapers everything, there will be no point in them doing anything to us. The world will know."

"But if something did, what about Jeff? Who would look after Jeff?"

"You know my sister would take him."

"I can't stand your sister," Patricia said.

"She has her faults," Edwin conceded. "But she'd do right by him, I'm sure of that. And not only that, there's—"

"Which terminal?" the taxi driver asked.

"Uh, Terminal One," Edwin said, raising his voice. He returned to whispering and said to his wife, "It's going to be okay. And we're doing the right thing. The Institute, Madam Director, they can't be allowed to do this. Dogs, well, dogs are one thing. But the way things were going . . ."

The taxi pulled up in front of the Arrivals level of the airport. The driver got out and helped them get their bags out of the trunk.

As Patricia and Edwin Conroy walked into the terminal, the driver reached into his pocket for his phone and entered a number.

"Daggert?" he said. "They're here."

05

After they had been on the road for two days, Harry thought it would be smart to get some more money. Buying food for the three of them, filling up the van with gas, and staying overnight in motels had only eaten up about half the cash he'd taken out a couple of days earlier, but he said it was better to have too much than too little. As they were driving through a small town, he spotted a bank with a cash machine visible just inside the door.

"Okay, guys," Harry said, pulling the van into an angled parking spot. "I won't be more than a couple of minutes."

As he was opening the door, Jeff, in the front passenger seat, said, "What about your disguise?"

Harry had one leg out the door. He was wearing a baseball cap and pulled the visor low over his forehead. "If I keep this down over my face, and tip my head forward, I don't think the cameras will get a very good look at me. Sticking that beard and stuff to my face, and pulling it off, is driving me crazy."

He got out and closed the door. Jeff and Chipper watched as he walked along the sidewalk towards the bank.

Look.

"Where?" Jeff asked.

Chipper was watching a police car moving slowly down the main street. The officer behind the wheel seemed to be glancing over at Harry.

"Uh oh," Jeff said.

The police cruiser wheeled into a spot and the officer slowly got out. He was definitely watching Harry as he got closer to the bank. But then he turned and looked at the van. The officer squinted, clearly trying to get a better look at who was inside.

"Oh no!" Jeff said. "He's looking right at us!"

This is bad.

"No kidding," Jeff said. "You think it's possible The Institute put out a description of us or something?"

Maybe.

Now the officer had turned the other way, just in time to see Harry go into the bank. The officer cocked his head to one side, as if Harry looked familiar to him. He walked slowly towards the door Harry had just disappeared through. When the officer reached it, he stopped, leaned towards the glass and peered inside. He made a visor out of his hand to reduce the glare.

"Oh no!" Jeff said again.

The officer reached for the door handle. He was heading into the bank.

"We have to do something," Jeff said.

Like what?

"Create some kind of diversion," the boy said.

Harry, taking a card from his wallet to insert into the cash machine, was clearly unaware of the approaching police officer.

Let me out.

"What are you going to do?" Jeff asked.

Just let me out.

Jeff decided there wasn't time to demand a detailed explanation. He opened the passenger door. Chipper leapt over him and down to the pavement.

Jeff got out, too, so that he could see what Chipper was going to do.

The dog darted out into the middle of the street. A car's brakes squealed.

"Chipper!" Jeff shouted.

But Chipper seemed to know what he was doing. He scooted across the street, then back again, then up the middle, along the painted dividing line. Cars continued to screech, horns blared.

Jeff glanced at the bank. The police officer had reached the bank and had his hand on the door, ready to open it, but had turned his head back towards the commotion.

Back in the street, Chipper continued to dash back and forth between cars until –

CRASH!

A pickup truck had rammed into the back of a low-slung sports car. The driver of the sports car jumped out, waving angrily at a woman behind the wheel of the truck.

"You idiot!" he shouted. "Watch where you're going!"

The woman put her head out the window and shouted back, "It was that stupid dog!"

As the police officer ran the half-block towards the accident scene, Jeff got out of the van, left the door open, and, using some parked cars as cover, headed for the bank.

Harry was coming out, shoving cash down into his front pocket, when Jeff got there.

"We have to go!" he said breathlessly.

"What?" Harry said. "What's going on?"

But Jeff, checking to make sure the police officer's attention was focused on the accident, was already high-tailing it back to the van, so Harry started running, too. By the time they reached the van, Chipper was back inside. Harry jumped behind the wheel and turned the key.

"That policeman looked like he was watching you!" Jeff said. "He saw you, and then he looked at us and then—"

"It's okay," Harry said, backing the van out of its spot, gears whining. "We're going."

Chipper, nose to the back window glass, watched

the officer trying to calm the angry sports-car driver as Harry pressed down hard on the accelerator.

Jeff glanced down at his phone as Chipper turned away from the window.

That was a close one.

"A little too close," Jeff said.

* * *

Tell me about Pepper.

Harry and Jeff and Chipper were sitting in a cheap motel room at the end of the day, the van hidden around back, when Chipper decided to ask about the dog Jeff once had.

The room had two double beds. Harry was stretched out on one, Jeff on the other, Chipper on the floor between them. The television was tuned in to the news   Harry's choice, not Jeff's – but the sound was muted.

Jeff smiled. "She was a great dog. I think the two of you would really hit it off. She lives with the Thomases now. I haven't seen her in over a year, not since my parents died and I had to go and live with Aunt Flo."

Does Pepper have software built into her?

"No. Pepper is just a regular dog."

I remember being a regular dog. I have dreams about being a regular dog.

Jeff patted the bed. Chipper sprang off the floor and snuggled in next to him, but not before having a

33

sniff of the now-empty pizza box sitting on the bed. Chipper had had two slices of extra cheese and pepperoni.

"Pepper never got to eat pizza for dinner," Jeff said.

Why not?

"My parents wouldn't have considered that proper dog food," Jeff said. "They said people food wasn't good for dogs."

But I love pizza.

"Yeah, well, who doesn't?" Jeff said. "I sure wish I could visit Pepper."

Harry raised his head. "That's not a good idea."

Jeff nodded wearily. "I know. But, Harry, what's the plan? Are we just going to wander around for ever, staying in a different motel every night?"

Harry sighed. "No, of course not."

"Then what are we going to do? School starts pretty soon. I'm supposed to go back. What am I going to do about school?"

"I think school is the least of your worries," Harry said.

I can teach you things.

"Right," Jeff said to Chipper. "*You're* going to be my teacher."

"He *is* pretty smart," Harry said. "Hey, Chipper, why does it rain?"

The dog looked at him and tilted his head to one side, then the other. Harry pointed to Jeff's phone and

Jeff tossed it over. Harry looked at the screen and read aloud what Chipper had to say.

"'Rain is caused when wet air rises up, then it condenses and turns into clouds, and when the clouds fill up with moisture and cannot hold any more it comes down as rain.'"

He tossed the phone back to Jeff and said, "You don't need to go to school. You've got a great teacher right here."

"My teacher can't be a dog," Jeff protested. "I can't have someone I have to go behind with a poop bag as a teacher."

If a dog could look offended, Chipper did.

"I don't mean that as an insult," the boy said. He sighed. "I can't believe I actually want to go back to school. Every other summer I just wanted to last for ever."

You want a normal life again.

"I guess I do," Jeff said. He shrugged. "I don't even know what normal is any more."

Chipper rested his snout on Jeff's knee sympathetically.

Harry swung his legs off the bed. He cleaned up the empty pizza box and drink cans and napkins and stuffed them into a wastebasket in the bathroom. When he came out, he said, "Will you guys be okay here for a minute while I get some air?"

"Yeah, sure," Jeff said.

35

Harry opened the motel room door and slipped out into the night. Chipper glanced up at Jeff.

I have to do my business.

"You need me to take you for a walk?"

No. And you know, if The Institute had sent me on missions, they would not have had someone, to quote you, going behind me with a poop bag.

"Yeah, well, I get that. That would kind of defeat the purpose of what you were designed to do, to sneak around and all."

Do we have to keep talking about this?

"No, I'm sorry. Let me get the door for you."

Jeff hopped off the bed and let Chipper out. "In case I fall asleep and don't see the phone, just scratch the door when you want back in."

Once outside, Chipper took in his surroundings. This motel was almost identical to the others they had stayed in: just off the road, the sounds of cars and trucks whooshing by in the night. About half the units were rented, with cars nosed up to the doors. Chipper did not know a lot about motels and hotels, but he had a feeling this place was not one of the nicer ones.

Chipper decided to slip around to the back of the motel to do what he had to do. He trotted down the length of the motel, rounded the corner, went down the side, and was about to make the final turn when he heard a familiar voice.

It was Harry.

Chipper edged his snout past the corner of the motel far enough for him to get a look at the man. Given that Chipper's real eyes had been replaced at The Institute with high-tech optical devices and a camera, it was relatively easy for him to see Harry, even though it was dark out.

He was alone, with a phone pressed to his ear. This was not the first time Chipper had wondered about the wisdom of Harry having a phone. Jeff had been careful to cut his own phone's connection to anything but Chipper. But, clearly, Harry's phone was capable of more. Jeff had asked him about this one day, and Harry had said it was one of those "burner" phones that couldn't be traced.

That seemed to calm Jeff's nerves, but Chipper was not convinced. He was close enough that he could hear some of what Harry was saying.

"Yeah, they're fine. Had some pizza. The dog loves pizza!" Harry laughed. "Two slices! I hope he doesn't throw up."

Then Harry went quiet, listening to whoever was at the other end of the call.

"Right," he said, then paused. "Yeah, he misses Pepper."

And then Harry said something that really made Chipper's ears perk up.

"We need to set up some kind of rendezvous where I can hand Jeff and the dog over to you."

Chipper actually felt a chill, and it wasn't even that cold out. He'd never felt a chill before that was not related to external temperature.

"Whenever you're ready," Harry said. "We'll stay on the move until then. Had a bit of a close call today when some cop gave us the once-over, but we got away. So I'll check in tomorrow or the next day. Can't say where I'll be. Just playing that by ear. But I've got lots of cash and can get more. Got lots of different cards in different names so they can't find us that way."

Chipper suddenly realised he should have been recording this. He had the capability. All he had to do was mentally activate the digital recording programme, and Harry's conversation, at least his side of it, would be picked up through receivers implanted in his ears.

But it looked as though Harry was nearly finished.

"Okay, bye," he said.

He put the phone back in his pocket.

Chipper pulled back, turned, and ran back around to the front of the motel.

Thinking.

What am I going to do? What am I going to tell Jeff?

06

Emily Winslow said, for not the first time, "We have to do *something*."

It was late evening, and she was standing on the dock while her father, John Winslow, sat in a small boat, changing a spark plug on an outboard motor that one of their guests needed first thing in the morning. She directed the beam of a flashlight on the motor so her father could see what he was doing.

"We've been through this a hundred times, Emily," he said. He had removed the cover on the motor so that he could service the engine, and he now grabbed a wrench to loosen the plug.

"But Jeff and Chipper are out there somewhere," she said. "He's my friend. I should be helping him. It's been three days. I haven't heard anything from them."

"And you're probably not going to do," her father said. "There's nothing we can do. This is not a normal situation. Those guys who came after him and the dog, they weren't your average law enforcement types.

They were from some agency that we've never even heard of. Anything we might do to help your friend could put us in a lot of danger. And even if we wanted to do something, what would it be? We don't know where he is. It's out of our hands."

Emily looked sternly at her father. "I don't understand you," she said.

He looked up from his work. "What do you mean?"

"You used to be a police officer. You cared about people in trouble."

John Winslow eyes saddened. "Oh, sweetheart, you know I care. But this . . . this is different. The smartest thing for us to do is keep our heads down. If those people get even a hint that we're going to do something, they'll be all over us in an instant."

"You never used to be afraid," Emily said.

"What I'm doing, I'm doing for you,' John said. "If it were just me, I'd be after those guys, helping your friend Jeff. But it's not that simple. If your mother were still with us, what would she say if I went charging off after those guys and something happened to me and you were left on your own? And that's not all. If I did go after those folks, they might come after *you*. I won't let that happen." He shook his head angrily. "No, I will not do that. I won't risk your life, not even for the lives of Jeff and that high-tech mutt of his."

Emily said, "It's like I don't even know you any more."

John Winslow tossed his wrench into the bottom of the boat and stepped out on to the dock. Emily swung the beam of the flashlight briefly past her father's face and saw that his cheeks were flushed. He made his hands into fists and placed them on his hips.

"Why do you think we're even still standing here?" he asked his daughter.

"What?"

"Why do you think we're even still alive?"

"What do you mean?"

"Look at what we know. We know about a very special dog, with very special powers. A dog from a secret project. And yet, we're still here, running this fishing camp. You know why?"

"Why?"

"Because they know we'll keep our mouths shut. They know that we know – well, that I know – that if we go flapping our gums about this to anyone, we're finished. They know that killing a retired cop might bring a little too much attention, but believe me, if they have to, they'd do it."

Emily had rarely seen her father this angry, but she did not back down. She stood face to face with him, her nose barely reaching his chin.

"One time, when I was little, you were hours late getting home from work, and I was worried about what might have happened to you with all those bad guys out in the world. You know what Mom said?"

Her father's jaw trembled ever so slightly. "What did she say?"

" 'Don't you worry about your daddy. He's not afraid of anybody.' Well, I guess she was wrong."

At which point Emily slapped the flashlight into his hand, turned on her heel, walked off the dock and headed for the house.

07

Madam Director called Daggert to her office for a late meeting. She was often in her office until midnight, or even later, and no one at The Institute dared go home before she did.

Daggert came through the doors and said, "You wanted to see me."

"Indeed," she said. "I have some exciting news."

Daggert looked unsure about whether to be excited. "Have they been found?"

Madam Director shook her head. "No. But this will help you with that."

Daggert waited.

"I'm assigning you a new team," Madam Director said.

"A new team?"

Daggert usually chose the people he worked with. It was Daggert who hired new recruits to the security department. Madam Director knew he would not like the idea of her picking the people he worked with.

"Yes," Madam Director said.

Daggert had been working with Bailey and Crawford. Bailey had shown herself to be incompetent. Crawford had also proved to be inept. But the truth was, they had all made mistakes, Daggert included, on their recent assignment to capture Chipper and bring him back to The Institute.

"With all due respect, Madam Director, I can pick my people."

"You picked Bailey and Crawford. How did that work out?"

"They made mistakes. So did I. But we'll get the job done."

"You certainly will," she said, icily.

She leaned forward and pressed a button on her desk again and said, "Send in Barbara and Timothy."

Daggert looked puzzled.

"Barbara and Timothy?" he said. "I know everyone in security and I don't know anyone by those names."

The door slid open.

Daggert had his eyes trained at shoulder level, but there was no one there for him to see. He angled his head downwards to better view his new team.

One was a dog, a Labrador retriever that came halfway up Daggert's thigh. It was wagging its tail.

The other was a child, a boy who looked no more than six years old.

"Uh," said Daggert.

The boy extended a hand upwards to Daggert. "Hello," he said in a childlike voice, that nevertheless sounded very self-assured. "My name is Timothy. You must be Daggert." Once Daggert had shaken his hand, the boy patted the dog's head. "And this is Barbara."

Daggert turned to look at Madam Director. "What . . ."

"Don't look so surprised, Daggert. You know what we do here."

Madam Director came out from behind her desk, a device the size of a phone in her hand. She briefly knelt down in front of Timothy and squeezed his shoulders. "Aren't you just my little man?"

"Yes," he said. "I am."

There was something about the boy's voice. Business-like. Slightly lacking in emotion.

Daggert said to Madam Director, "This was done very quickly. I didn't think any . . . I knew we had other canines ready to go, but I didn't know there were . . ."

"Yes," Madam Director said. "We moved ahead very quickly with young Timothy. I'm very pleased with the progress. His time with you will be something of a test for him. And Barbara here is every bit the dog you've been hunting, except she does not get distracted."

Then Madam Director said, "Barbara. Look at me."

The dog raised its head and locked its artificial eyes on her. At that moment, the director pressed a button

45

in the device she'd been holding. Suddenly, a mouse shot out from under her desk and scurried across the marble floor. Except it was not a mouse, but a tiny toy designed to look exactly like one.

Barbara's eyes shifted, for a mere fraction of a second, in the direction of the mouse, but she did not move. She did not chase it, nor did she appear tempted.

"I think we know what H-1094 would have done, don't we?" Madam Director said. "That mouse would have distracted him completely. And now, you, Timothy. Why don't you impress me?"

Timothy stood at attention, waiting.

"Timothy, what are they talking about in the next room?"

Daggert's expression seemed to say, *What?*

On the other side of the wall of Madam Director's office was one of the control rooms at The Institute. It was there that many employees sat at computers all day, tracking the movements of The Institute's operatives – human and not-so-human. There were people in that room, right now, helping Daggert search for Harry Green and the boy and the dog by listening in on phones, tracking bank transactions and checking photos from highway cameras.

Timothy cocked his head slightly to one side and said, "Someone is saying, 'I wonder what soup they are serving in the cafeteria today.'"

Daggert said, "That is pretty amazing, I admit, being able to hear through walls or a door, but—"

"Wait," said Timothy. "There's more. Someone is saying, 'That Madam Director, she's the nastiest piece of work ever.'"

Madam Director's eyes narrowed. "Oh, really? Timothy, are you able to identify who said that by accessing our voice recognition files?"

The boy nodded. He stood motionless for several seconds, as if he had gone into some kind of stasis.

"It is Wilkins."

"Wilkins?" Daggert said. "Which one is – oh, right, Wilkins. I keep thinking his name is Watson."

"So, that's what Wilkins thinks of me," Madam Director said, her voice trailing off. "Well, that's it. The three of you are dismissed."

Timothy looked up at Daggert without expression. "I look forward to working with you."

And Barbara said, "Woof."

"We'll sort out your communications with Barbara shortly," Madam Director said. "We have made some improvements in that area, too. Off you go."

Without another word, Daggert, Timothy and Barbara headed for the door. But once the boy and the dog had left, Daggert held back.

"Madam Director," he said tentatively.

"Yes, Daggert?"

"The boy, Timothy."

"Yes?"

"How old is he?"

"He's six."

Daggert ran a hand over his mouth. "Just . . . a child."

Madam Director's eyes became slits. "Is there a problem, Daggert?"

Abruptly, he shook his head. "No, of course not. No problem at all. I'll be on my way."

Madam Director said, "Daggert?"

"Yes?"

"Would you send Wilkins in?"

08

Entering the airport terminal, Edwin Conroy said to his wife, "We have to get our boarding passes."

They approached the ticket agent and Edwin told her their flight number, presenting photo ID for himself and his wife. She stood nervously to one side as the agent printed out their passes.

Once he had them in hand, Edwin said, "Okay, we're good to go. Gate forty-one."

"That man over there," Patricia said.

"What man?"

"Don't be obvious about looking, but he's over there by the newspapers. He's just been standing there, not looking at the magazines or anything. I think he's watching us."

Edwin slowly turned his head, pretending to look off in another direction, but scanning the newspaper stand.

"The one in the grey suit?" he said.

"Yes," Patricia said, leaning into her husband, her back to the man.

"Looks to me like he's reading the paper, Patsy. Look, I get why you're paranoid. I am, too. But I think we're going to be – hang on."

"What?" Patricia huddled even closer to her husband.

"It's not the man I'm worried about."

"What are you talking about?" she said.

"Turn around slowly and look."

Patricia broke free of Edwin and viewed the scores of people moving through the terminal. Families, businesspeople, all dragging luggage behind them. Some, fearful of missing their flights, were running flat out.

"What am I looking at?" she asked.

"Way over there by the coffee place."

Patricia looked. "I see half a dozen people. Which one are you wondering about?"

"I'm not wondering about any of them. I'm wondering about the dog."

Patricia took a sharp intake of breath. "Oh no."

It was a German Shepherd, sitting just outside the airport coffee shop, looking in their direction.

"I don't see a leash or anything," she said. "It's not wearing one of those harnesses, like it would be if it was a guide dog."

"If it belonged to someone, you'd think it would be tied to something."

"Do you remember a dog like that at The Institute?"

Edwin tried to think. "There were so many. I know there were a couple of German Shepherds, but I can't tell for sure whether that was one of them."

"Let's head to our gate, see if he follows us," Patricia said.

They started walking, each wheeling a bag behind them. When they had gone no more than ten paces, Edwin glanced over his shoulder.

"Is he following?" Patricia asked.

"He's gone," he said. "I don't see him. No, wait. There he is. He's walking in our direction."

"Oh no," Patricia said. "They're out to get us. I know it."

"The man in the grey suit, I don't see him, either."

"I don't like your sister," Patricia said.

"What?"

"I don't want her raising Jeff."

"Let's not get ahead of ourselves here, Patsy."

They kept walking. In two minutes, they had reached Gate 41. People were already lining up to board the plane. Edwin and Patricia each held a boarding pass and photo ID – passports in their case, even though they didn't need them for a flight that was within the country.

Edwin took another look back.

"There he is," he said.

The dog was strolling past the gates when a uniformed male security official shouted: "Sam!" The dog turned, saw the man, wagged his tail and sprinted towards him.

"It's nothing," Edwin said. "It's probably a dog trained to sniff out drugs. He works here! And I still don't see that guy in the grey suit, either. It's going to be okay. We're going to get on that plane and get out of here."

The man checking boarding passes scanned theirs and said, "Have a nice flight."

Edwin and Patricia put away their passports and headed down the tunnel-like jetbridge towards the plane.

Chipper scooted back to the motel room door and started scratching frantically. Then he barked.

The door swung open quickly. "What's the matter, Chipper?" Jeff asked. The dog slipped into the room and leapt up on the bed. "Did you do what you had to do?"

Chipper was very much thinking about what he *should* do.

Clearly, Harry Green was up to something. He was on the phone with somebody discussing Jeff and Chipper himself. Who was Harry talking to?

Chipper was about to communicate a thought to Jeff when the door opened and in stepped Harry.

"It gets cool out there at night," he said.

"You almost need a jacket," Jeff said. "Which kinda brings up another point. I didn't exactly have time to pack a bag when we left my aunt's place. I know we stopped and got a toothbrush and things, but pretty soon I'm going to need to get some extra clothes." He sniffed his armpit. "Pretty soon, you're not going to want me in the van with you."

"I hear ya," Harry said. "Tell you what. Tomorrow, we'll hit a mall and get some basics. Underwear, a couple of shirts, some more jeans. And we'll find a coin laundry and wash what we've been wearing. Does that sound like a plan?"

"I guess," Jeff said. "But it's not really a plan for the bigger picture."

Chipper's head went back and forth, following the conversation.

"I know, I know," Harry Green said. "I've been giving that a lot of thought."

"What's your idea?" Jeff asked hopefully.

"Well, I haven't really pulled it together quite yet. But I'm working on it, no doubt about it."

Jeff gave Harry a sceptical look for several seconds. "You don't seem very – I don't know – worried about not having a plan."

Harry grinned at Jeff. "No sense losing your head over these things. You have to be methodical. Plan carefully. Consider your options."

"But it's not like you've ever been in a situation like this before," Jeff said.

"You're right about that."

Now Jeff looked even more sceptical. "What did you really do before you retired?"

"What? I told you. I did construction work. Built houses, renovations, that kind of thing."

"And for that you kept a backpack full of disguises?"

"I *explained* that to you, Jeff. Come on, what's going on here?" Harry looked wounded. "It's like you don't trust me or something."

Jeff's suspicious expression faded. "Sorry. I didn't mean that."

Harry motioned for Jeff to sit on the edge of the bed, sat down next to him, put his arm around him and gave him a quick squeeze. "Hey, what's wrong? You think I'm not trying to do my best for you?"

Jeff nodded slowly. "I know. I know you are."

Chipper looked at the phone Jeff held in his hand, wondering whether, if he were to send a message, Harry would see it. But what would he say?

If Harry was up to something, if he was working against them, and Chipper did something that let Harry know he was on to him, would that put Jeff and him in more danger? There was no way to know what Harry might do. And while Chipper had some tricks up his furry sleeve – not the least of which was the ability to make an ear-piercing noise, as he'd done when that Daggert character had Jeff and him cornered – what then? He and Jeff were in the middle of nowhere. What were they supposed to do once they got beyond the door of that motel room?

If it were just himself, Chipper thought, he could make a run for it, just like he had done when he escaped The Institute. But this time, he'd be bringing Jeff with him, and that wouldn't be nearly as easy.

Was it better to let things play out a little longer, to see what Harry was planning? See who he was working for? Was it possible this was a huge trick, that Harry was actually working *for* The Institute at the same time as he was pretending to protect them from it? Or could he be working for another government, or secret agency, that wanted Chipper's technology?

Jeff had glanced at his phone several times. He looked at Chipper and said, "You've been awfully quiet lately."

The dog looked at him, unsure what to say.

I guess I am tired.

"Yeah, well, we all are," Jeff said. "Harry, I was looking at the map and where you think we might go next. We're going to be driving right past the town where I used to live."

"Yeah?" Harry said. "So?"

"Could we, like, drive past my house? I'd like to show Chipper where I grew up. You'd like to see that, wouldn't you, boy?"

Sure.

Harry was considering the request. "If you're thinking of having a visit with Pepper, that's way too risky."

"Just a drive-by," Jeff said. "No stopping. I promise."

"And what if you see your dog playing in the yard? What then? You're gonna want to stop and get out. That's when we could get spotted."

Jeff's lip trembled at the thought of seeing Pepper. "Well, if we did see her, we could drive around the block to make sure no one was following us and—"

"You see?" Harry said, shaking his head with annoyance. "You see what you're trying to do? You're all, 'Harry, all I want to do is drive down the street. Oh, Harry, maybe I could just get out for a second and throw a ball for my dog. Oh, Harry, maybe I could visit all my friends.'"

Harry dropped his head wearily before looking back up. "That's a good way for us to get spotted."

Then Jeff did something neither Harry nor Chipper was expecting.

He started to cry.

He put his face in his hands and bawled.

"Aw, kid," Harry said, putting his hand on the boy's back. "Aw, don't do that."

Chipper nuzzled his snout on top of Jeff's knees and whimpered, as though crying along with him.

"I just wanted to see my house," Jeff said. "Sometimes . . . I'm afraid I'm going to forget."

"Forget what?" Harry asked.

Jeff, teary-eyed, tried to explain. "What if I can't remember all the things that mattered to me? If I'm on the run with you and Chipper for ever I'm scared I'll forget the life I used to have. I'll forget my house and I'll forget my mom and dad and I'll forget I ever even had a dog named Pepper. I can't even believe I might feel sad about this, but I might even forget about living with Aunt Flo." He paused. "You think she's okay?"

Harry nodded slowly. "I bet Emily's dad will be checking in on her."

Jeff's lips trembled into half a smile. He looked at Chipper and said, "What do you think?"

The dog took a moment to reply.

I would never forget you. No matter what.

10

Daggert, little Timothy and Barbara, who was wagging her tail, were in the central control room, hovering over Wilkins. He was sitting at a computer, tapping away.

"How's it going, Watson?" Daggert asked.

Wilkins stopped, craned his head around and looked with annoyance at Daggert. "It's Wilkins."

"Sorry. I'm told you have a simple way for Barbara here to talk to me."

Wilkins looked at the dog. "Right." He opened a drawer next to his keypad and brought out a shiny black plastic box. He opened the lid, revealing what appeared to be a tiny earpiece.

"Just slip this in. It's all ready to go."

Daggert picked it up between his thumb and forefinger, then carefully inserted it into his right ear. "Like this?"

"Yup." Wilkins looked at the dog. "Give it a try."

Barbara looked up at Daggert. In his ear, he heard, *"Nice to be working with you, Daggert."*

The voice, while slightly robotic, was crystal clear. "Uh, nice to be working with you Barbara." To Wilkins, he said, "So I just leave this thing in my ear all the time?"

"That's right. There's something else you need to know about Barbara."

"What's that?"

"Don't get all kissy-face with her."

"I don't get all kissy-face with anyone," Daggert said.

"Yeah, well, I believe that," Wilkins said. "But you need to know, Barbara's saliva is treated with a sedative. She's immune to it herself, but if she licks you on the face, you'll be fast asleep in no time at all."

Daggert looked at Barbara. She ran her tongue down one side of her jaw and then the other.

"Noted," Daggert said. "Now, what success are you having tracking down the Conroy kid and the dog?"

"Everyone's on it," Wilkins said with frustration. "There was one possible sighting of this Harry Green character, but the police officer who saw him was distracted by a traffic accident. Green seems to have had practice dodging the authorities."

Timothy edged in close enough to reach the keyboard. Daggert couldn't help noticing that the boy's chin barely cleared it.

"Hey there, little man, don't touch that," Wilkins said. To Daggert, he said, "What is this? Take Your Kid to Work Day? I don't see anyone else bringing in their little snots." He grinned. "Somehow, I've never seen you as a father, Daggert."

"He's not my kid," Daggert said. "He's my new partner. Him and Barbara here."

"Oh, right," Wilkins said, looking at Timothy. "Our latest technical achievement."

The golden retriever was looking at Wilkins as though he were a rare steak.

"*I do not like this man.*"

"Me neither," Daggert said, responding to the dog's voice in his ear.

"What did you say?" Wilkins asked.

"Sorry. I was talking to Barbara."

Timothy had his hands on the mouse and was clicking away at Wilkins' screen.

"Hey!" he protested. "Knock it off."

Timothy had accessed the video feeds of a major highway system. "Have you been looking at these? If you enter in a picture of the van, even if it has different plates, it should get picked up here."

Wilkins took a long look at the boy. "I know how to do my job."

"Do you?" Timothy asked. He did some more computer clicking. "There, what about that?"

Everyone, even Barbara, looked at the screen. It showed a van that looked very much like Harry Green's passing through an intersection.

"That . . . does look like it," Wilkins said. "But we can't be sure."

"I thought I could see a dog in there."

"Barbara thinks she sees H-1094," Daggert said.

Wilkins studied the screen and scoffed. "I don't think so. Anyway, there are a lot of vans like that on the road. And that isn't the right licence plate."

The boy began tapping away on the computer at lightning speed. "Look at that," he said. "That plate was reported stolen off another car three days ago."

"Oh, yeah, so it was," Wilkins said.

Under his breath, Daggert said, "Wow."

The kid's abilities were astounding, no doubt about it. But Daggert, for reasons he did not quite understand, felt sad more than impressed. He thought back to what skills he'd mastered when he was Timothy's age. Riding a bike came to mind.

"Okay," Wilkins said, "that might be something I can work with. Thanks, kid, but I'll take it from here."

Timothy said to Daggert, "Isn't there something you have to tell him?"

Daggert said. "Madam Director would like to see you."

"Me? Why?"

Daggert shrugged. "I guess you'll just have to go and talk to her and find out."

Wilkins took a deep breath, then said, "Okay, then, I'll see you in a while."

"Maybe," Daggert said.

As Wilkins walked off, Timothy hopped up into his chair, then looked at Daggert. He said, "You know, you're going about this all wrong."

"Uh, sorry?"

"You're hunting all over the place for the boy and H-1094. And even though we now know they were at that intersection a couple of days ago, we still have no idea where they are right now. They could be zigzagging all over the country."

"Listen to Timothy. He is on to something."

"Okay," Daggert said. He definitely did not like being talked to this way by a six year old, and he definitely wanted to dig out that earpiece.

"Instead of us trying to find them," Timothy said, "it would make more sense to bring them to us."

Daggert blinked. He looked at the next work station, where there was an empty chair, wheeled it over, and sat down.

"And how do you propose we do that?"

"We don't go after *them*. We go after something else that *matters* to them."

"What did you have in mind?"

"I have two suggestions," Timothy said.

Edwin and Patricia continued to walk down the jetbridge to board their plane. The floor thumped beneath their feet with each step. Edwin was ahead of Patricia, since the tunnel was too narrow to walk side by side and still allow room for anyone walking the other way.

Edwin was looking towards the open door of the plane when he heard Patricia say, "Nuts!"

He stopped and turned.

Patricia had lost her grip on the bag's handle and it had fallen to the floor. Her handbag had been resting on top of it, so it had gone down too, spilling several items. Edwin put his carry-on bag into a standing position and went back to help his wife, who was already on her knees, stuffing things back into her handbag.

"I'm such an idiot."

"Here, let me," Edwin said. He grabbed a bottle of nail polish that had rolled two feet away. Other passengers stepped around them on the way to the plane. Patricia looked up, mumbling apologies.

A man in coveralls, coming from the plane, walked past them as he headed for the gate. He looked like a maintenance person. Patricia viewed him for no more than a fraction of a second as he went by.

"I think we got everything," Edwin said, scanning the floor.

"Edwin," Patricia whispered. She stood, and tipped her head back towards the gate. "That man."

"What man?"

"Heading back into the terminal. In the worker's uniform." She held her hand worriedly over her mouth. "I think . . . I think I recognised him. But I could be wrong."

"Who do you think he was?"

"That awful man, what's his name . . . Taggert?"

"Taggert?"

"No. Daggert. Head of security."

Edwin looked instantly alarmed. "Are you sure?"

"I . . . think so."

"What would he be doing—"

Edwin looked at the open door of the plane, then back to the gate, debating whether to run after the man. But now he was gone. And once he was in the terminal, Edwin would never find him.

Patricia said, "I'm just so on edge, so nervous, maybe I'm getting completely paranoid. I think everyone is watching us."

Edwin nodded his head comfortingly. "Everything's going to be okay. Like you said, we're on edge."

Patricia slung her handbag over her shoulder and grabbed the handle of her carry-on bag. Edwin went back for his.

The plane's open door beckoned to them.

12

The day after Chipper had seen Harry on the phone behind the motel, the two of them and Jeff were back on the road and driving through another small town when Harry suddenly pulled over and stopped the car.

"What are you doing?" asked Jeff.

"We need to ditch this van," Harry said. "I know we've got different plates on it, but I don't think that's enough." He pointed to a van on the other side of the road with a 'For Sale' sign on it. "Maybe, if the price was right, the person selling that van might not be too fussy about a proper title and plates and things like that."

Jeff had not noticed the van for sale until Harry had pointed it out. It was one of those Volkswagen camper vans, the bottom half red and the top half white, and judging by the rusted fenders and hubcaps, it was decades old. It had a raised part in the roof that could be cranked up higher to allow occupants to stand. A cardboard sign had been tucked under the wiper. It read BEST OFFER.

Harry got out of the van and went up to the ramshackle house it was parked next to, which looked as though it had needed a new coat of paint since before paint was invented. He knocked on the door.

Jeff noticed that some words had appeared on his phone.

I want to ask you something now that we are alone.

Jeff's eyebrows went up. "Uh, okay."

Have you been wondering any more about Harry?

"What do you mean?" Jeff asked.

The other day you asked what I thought about him. Are you still wondering?

Jeff shrugged. "I keep thinking there's stuff we don't know about him."

Like what?

"All these disguises he's got yet he's supposed to be some retired construction guy. It doesn't seem to add up." Jeff shook his head. "Maybe it does, I don't know."

The dog had nothing to say for a few moments.

"Something on your mind?" Jeff asked. "You're not very chatty. I feel like you're holding back."

I want you to be safe. That is why I wanted to find you.

"And you did that. What's on your mind?"

Chipper hesitated. He looked out the window and watched as Harry talked to a bearded man in a plaid shirt and frayed jeans. The man with the beard nodded enthusiastically as Harry handed over some cash. In return, the man gave him a key.

We can talk later.

"No, tell me."

I think Harry Green was staying at Flo's Cabins for a reason.

"Yeah, to go fishing."

No. To keep an eye on you.

"What? That's nuts."

Harry walked over to the van he'd just bought, got behind the wheel and inserted the key. The engine rattled noisily to life. Smoke spewed out of the back end, where the engine was located. He took the BEST OFFER sign out of the window, got out and opened the doors. Then he started walking back towards them.

"What do you mean, he was there to keep an eye on me? Why would he do that? How could he even know about me?"

Harry was almost to the car.

Not now.

"No, hold on, you can't just bring up something like this and—"

Do not say anything in front of Harry.

"But—"

The driver's door opened. Harry's smile went from ear to ear. "We got us some new wheels, folks!"

"It looks like a piece of junk," Jeff said.

"Indeed it does. But it runs, and that's all that matters. It's even got a little fridge, and a table to eat at, and a bed in the back in case someone wants to take a nap!"

He started up the van and pulled it over alongside the other one. "Let's transfer everything over."

They didn't have all that much stuff, so it didn't take long. Then Harry told them to wait while he drove the van they had been using deep into the woods behind the seller's house. Minutes later he came running back and got behind the wheel of their new/old vehicle.

"Had to give the guy a few extra hundreds to let me hide the old one on his property." Harry threw the van into gear and pulled out on to the road. "On we go! And we'll be going past your old neighbourhood within the hour, Jeff! I think we can take a quick spin through!"

Jeff should have been excited, but all he could think about was what Chipper had said. There was something about Harry that was not right. Jeff felt it too. But if he and Chipper couldn't count on Harry, what would they do?

13

Daggert was having a hard time adjusting to working with one partner who was not human, and another who was not old enough to drive. It was, quite frankly, embarrassing. If it were just Barbara, the dog, riding with him in his black SUV, that would be okay. Plenty of people in law enforcement and other security work brought dogs along when they were out in the field.

But a kid?

Of course, Daggert fully understood the importance of testing The Institute's latest invention, and that's what Timothy really was: an invention. While The Institute had several children in various stages of development, Timothy was the first to perform well enough to be put into service. His high-tech software additions had merged well with his biological functions, and it had all been accomplished in a matter of days.

The Institute knew that children would attract no more attention than dogs when it came to spying.

Who'd ever suspect a little boy could be soaking up all that was going on around him and sending the information back to a secret agency? But with some of the children, they had run into problems similar to those they'd had with Chipper. During training, that dog had abandoned trailing an enemy agent to pursue a rabbit. One of the children The Institute had been working with, a little girl named Peggy, loved cats. In test runs, Peggy would interrupt her mission if she saw a kitten. She'd much rather cuddle a kitty than follow a suspected terrorist back to his hideout.

Daggert knew all this, and knew he had a job to do. But that didn't mean he always liked it. Daggert was, as the saying went, a company man. He was loyal to his employer and Madam Director. He followed orders. Back when Chipper escaped, Daggert was prepared to do whatever Madam Director wanted. Grab the dog, kill it if necessary, get rid of that Conroy boy. And Daggert had had no problem bringing down that plane to get rid of the boy's parents when it looked as though they were going to tell the world about The Institute's latest project.

But there was something about Timothy that troubled Daggert.

Who was this boy? Who had he been before The Institute filled him with hardware and software? What kind of child would he have been if he'd not been so drastically altered?

Did Timothy fully understand what had been done to him? Did he understand what had been taken away?

No, don't be thinking that way, Daggert told himself. *Do not question the mission. Don't give voice to your doubts, even if they're only voiced in your head.*

These thoughts ran through Daggert's mind as he pulled the shiny, black, almost entirely windowless van he was driving into the parking lot of a McDonald's. He, Timothy and Barbara had just completed the first part of a two-part assignment, and needed something to eat.

As Daggert and Timothy got out of the car, Daggert said to Barbara, who was wagging her tail, "You stay here."

In his ear, Daggert heard Barbara's response.

"Okay. Can you bring me back a burger?"

Daggert sighed. "Yeah, sure. You want fries with that?"

"Oh yes!"

He shook his head. This was what it had come to. Taking fast food orders from a dog. If Barbara was so smart, let *her* get behind the wheel and do the drive-through, he thought. As Daggert closed and locked the van, he could hear barking inside.

He went into the restaurant and lined up for food, Timothy at his side. "What do you want to eat?" Daggert asked.

Having all sorts of circuitry jammed into him clearly had done nothing to curb Timothy's appetite. He wanted a burger, an extra large order of French fries and the biggest chocolate milkshake on the menu. Daggert ordered a salad and a coffee. They sat down across from each other. The first thing Timothy did was lift off the top of the bun and examine the condiments. When he spotted two slices of pickle, he dug them out of the soupy mix of mustard, relish and ketchup.

"I hate pickles," he said, dropping them on the plastic tray and licking the other condiments off his fingers.

"Yeah," Daggert said. "Me too." He picked up a paper napkin and handed it to the boy. "Did they not teach you how to use one of these?"

Timothy used the napkin to further clean his fingers, then rubbed it across his mouth. He replaced the top of the bun and dug into his food as if he hadn't eaten for months.

"So," Daggert said, "what's your story?"

"What do you want to know?" Timothy said, stuffing his mouth with fries.

"Who are your parents? Or, who *were* your parents? They okay with what you've . . . been turned into?"

Timothy took a break from chewing to study Daggert. "I think that might be classified."

"It's okay," Daggert said. "We're partners, so we can tell each other anything."

"I don't have any parents."

"Yeah, well, Timothy, you may be a stunning example of what science can do, but I'm pretty sure

74

you were not made from scratch in a laboratory. Who are your mother and father?"

"I don't know."

"What do you mean, you don't know?"

"Right after I was born, six years ago, I was put up for adoption."

"Oh," Daggert said. "Do you know anything at all about your parents?"

"I know that my mother was all alone, and didn't feel she could raise me."

"What about your father?" Daggert asked.

Timothy shrugged.

Daggert said, "So how long were you at the adoption agency before they placed you with a family?"

"I was not placed with a family."

"No one wanted to adopt you?"

"I didn't say that," Timothy said. He slipped the straw into his mouth and took a long draw on the milkshake. "I was adopted, but not placed with a family. It was like going to another adoption agency."

Daggert guessed The Institute must have been working on this project for years. They'd take in infants, raise them and, when they were old enough, they'd be enhanced for The Institute's own ends.

"And then what happened?" he asked.

Timothy said, "Then one day, they brought me to meet Madam Director. She said she was going to make me really, really smart."

"And that's just what she did."

Timothy nodded.

Daggert asked, "Do you like being really, really smart?

Timothy hesitated. "Sometimes, there's too much stuff happening in my head. It's like having a million TV channels going on in there at once."

Daggert nodded slowly. "That doesn't sound so great."

Timothy shrugged. "Do you know the first line of 'The Serenity Prayer'?"

"What line?"

" 'God grant me the serenity to accept the things I cannot change.' " Then Timothy went back to stuffing burger into his mouth.

There's something funny about this kid that has nothing to do with his software, Daggert thought. He couldn't figure out what it was.

"How do you even know something like that?" Daggert asked.

Timothy offered another shrug. "I know all kinds of things. What about you?" he asked.

"What about me?"

"Do you have any kids?"

"No," Daggert said. "I don't like kids."

Timothy had no reaction to that. "How about a wife or a girlfriend?"

"No," he replied.

"Are you gay?"

Was this kid really just six?

"No. It's just, having kids, or a wife or a girlfriend – or a boyfriend, if I were gay – would complicate my life. I'm devoted to The Institute. I don't need any distractions."

"Oh," Timothy said. "I guess that's what my life will be like."

Daggert nodded his head slowly. "Yeah, I suppose it will be."

Timothy studied him for another moment, then went back to his milkshake.

When they were finished eating, and dumping their garbage into the trash bin, Daggert hung on to Timothy's straw.

14

Jeff normally liked sleepovers. He especially liked sleepovers with his friend, Kevin Thomas. But he hadn't been looking forward to this one.

The kind of sleepovers Jeff liked were the ones you could walk away from. If you went over to a friend's house, hoping to have lots of fun, but found that you weren't having any fun at all, it was comforting to know that you could call your parents, have them pick you up, and go home.

You might get sick. Or you and your supposedly-best-friend-in-the-whole-world might end up having a big fight over something. If there happened to be a second guest at the sleepover, he and your friend might gang up against you, and squeeze you out of the activities. Like, play video games all night when there were only two controllers, so you ended up in the kitchen with your friend's mom, eating brownies and feeling sorry for yourself. That was when you'd call your mom or dad to come and pick you up. Even *if you weren't sick, you'd say you thought you were going to throw up, and you were probably running a fever, too.*

But if Jeff didn't feel well tonight, or had a disagreement with his friend, Kevin, he wasn't going to be able to go back home. Not with his parents flying out of town to some drug industry conference or whatever it was. His parents didn't really talk that much about what they did, and it sounded pretty boring anyway, so Jeff didn't ask. A couple of times over the years, he had asked his parents about going to work with them one day, just to see where they did whatever they did, and they always said the same thing.

"Oh yes, one of these days, that'd be fun. But it's a pretty boring place, Jeff. You'd probably hate it."

So he stopped asking.

At least he was able to bring Pepper with him to the sleepover. Pepper would sleep on the bed with Kevin and him, right in the middle. Kevin loved Pepper, too, so it was okay.

Once Jeff had tossed his overnight bag containing clothes and pyjamas and a toothbrush and a comb into Kevin's room, they went to the basement and played video games for about two hours.

At one point, Kevin's mother, who was pretty cool for a really old person, popped down with crisps and

Coke and said, "Your eyes are going to go square if you play those games much longer."

That was when Jeff told Kevin he wanted to show him some tricks he had taught Pepper. They put the controllers aside and Jeff called to his dog, who had fallen asleep on the carpet.

Pepper jumped up, drawn to a crisp Kevin offered her. Pepper snatched it from his hand and chomped it down. It was clear she wanted another, and Kevin gave her one.

"Okay, girl," Jeff said to his black and white border collie. "Let's show Kevin here what you can do." To Kevin, he said, "They say that the border collie is one of the smartest breeds."

"I've heard that," Kevin said. He reached for his controller, shut down the game system, and switched the television to a cable channel showing a movie about an alien killing everyone on a spaceship.

Jeff got on his knees and had Pepper stand directly in front of him. He wanted the dog to look him in the eye, but every few seconds she gazed longingly at the bowl of crisps.

"Okay, Pepper, look at me." He held his hand out before her. "Now shake!"

Pepper did nothing.

"Shake! Give me a paw! Shake hands!"

Pepper did nothing.

Kevin said, "Good trick, dude."

"Just wait," Jeff said. "Pepper, we worked on this before, remember?"

Pepper looked at him with her deep, brown eyes.

"Now, shake."

Again, Pepper did nothing.

"Okay," Jeff said, undefeated. "Let's try this. Play dead."

Pepper took a step forward and licked Jeff's face.

"No, no," Jeff said, pushing her away. "Play dead."

When Pepper did not fall over lifelessly, Jeff demonstrated. He clutched his heart dramatically and collapsed on the rug.

"Like that!" Jeff said. "Dead! You can do it."

Pepper stood over him and licked his face some more.

"Man, I hate to say this, but your dog is dumb," Kevin said. "I love her, but she's dumb."

"She's not dumb," Jeff protested. "She's distracted by the crisps."

"Yeah, right."

"Come on, Pepper, play dead for me, please."

Pepper turned her attention from Jeff to Kevin, deciding his face needed a tongue bath too. Kevin hugged the dog around the neck.

"She may be totally stupid," Kevin said, "but she's still a nice dog. I'd love a dog like Pepper." He looked beyond Pepper at the TV. The alien was creeping down one of the space-station hallways.

Jeff said, "She knew how to do all this stuff at my house, I swear."

"Don't worry about it. A dog doesn't – hey, grab the remote."

"What?" said Jeff.

"Grab the remote, turn it up."

Jeff reached for the remote and was upping the volume even before he could see what was on the screen. A grim-faced newscaster filled the screen.

"—rupt this programme to bring you breaking news. Details are just starting to come in that a passenger jet heading to Boston from New Jersey has gone down in the Atlantic Ocean, not far offshore."

Jeff stared at the screen, his stomach slowly starting to roll over.

"Witnesses along the waterfront who captured video with their cell phones say they saw a bright light in the sky, almost like fireworks, and then parts of the plane came falling down."

There followed grainy video of bright lights in the sky going in all different directions.

"No," Jeff said quietly. "No."

A light appeared at the top of the stairs that led down to the basement. It was Kevin's mother, her face full of horror. Jeff could hear that an upstairs television was also on.

"It doesn't seem possible that anyone could have survived an explosion like this."

Pepper walked over in front of the television, lay down on her side, and pretended to be dead.

15

"Remember," said Harry, sitting behind the wheel of the van, "we're not stopping, we're not getting out, we're not talking to anybody. I don't even want to slow down that much. Are we clear?'

"Got it," Jeff said.

Understood.

They had taken a detour off the main highway to drive through Jeff's old neighbourhood. Chipper had his nose pressed to the glass to get a better look at where Jeff had grown up, but he had other things on his mind.

"Have you even been back since you went to live with your aunt?" Harry asked Jeff, who was sitting next to him up front.

Jeff shook his head. He'd asked his aunt several times if he could go, but she'd always put him off.

Chipper listened to the conversation, but he was still thinking about the phone call Harry'd had behind the motel. He had not told Jeff about it, and he'd done nothing to let on to Harry that he knew the man was not being straight with them.

Jeff, realising they were close, said, "Turn up here! That's my street!"

Harry put on the turn signal and made a right. "Nice street, Jeff. Which was your house?"

"There, on the left," he said, pointing. Chipper had taken up a spot between them, resting his head on the dash.

"Maybe someday," Jeff said wistfully, "I can move back here. When I'm grown up, maybe I could even buy back my parents' house from whoever owns it now. Or even before that, maybe I could live at Kevin's house. That's it, right across from mine. Maybe they could sort of adopt me. If it was okay, you know, with Aunt Flo. Like, she's my legal guardian, but maybe that could be changed."

Harry said, "Yeah, well, hard to say how things will turn out . . ."

As the van slowly rolled past Jeff's and Kevin's houses, Jeff looked half a block ahead.

Suddenly, he saw something that got his attention.

Jeff said, "Look! It's Kevin!"

He'd spotted his friend standing by a wooden telephone pole. Kevin had a sheaf of paper in one hand and what looked like a staple gun in the other. He was attaching a flyer to the pole. Jeff quickly glanced up and down the street and noticed other poles with similar notices stuck to them.

"What's that?" Jeff asked. "What's he putting up? It looks like a picture and some words."

Chipper put his paws on the dash and rose up.

I can see it.

"What does it say?" Jeff asked.

I think you should really see it for yourself.

"Hang on a second," Harry said. "Jeff, you're not getting out and talking to your friend. Look, he doesn't know me. I can ask him what it's about."

Harry stopped the van, left the engine running, and got out.

"Could you tell me what it said?" Jeff asked Chipper.

Just wait.

They watched as Harry ambled up the sidewalk. By the time he got to Kevin, the boy had moved on to the next pole. Harry struck up a conversation, chatted briefly. Kevin handed Harry one of the sheets.

Harry walked back to the van and got inside, the sheet of paper clutched in his hand.

"What is it?" Jeff asked.

Harry grimaced and handed it over. It featured a big picture of a dog that looked very much like Chipper. Beneath the picture was the word PEPPER.

Above it were these words:

MISSING DOG!
HAVE YOU
SEEN ME?

86

IF SO, CALL
MY OWNERS!

And that was followed by a phone number and an email address.

"Oh no!" Jeff said. "I have to talk to Kevin!"

"No!" Harry said.

But before he could grab Jeff's arm, the boy was out of the passenger door, with Chipper bounding after him. Jeff ran up the street.

"Kevin! Kevin!"

Kevin whirled around and his jaw dropped at the sight of his long-lost friend and Chipper.

"Jeff?!"

Kevin ran towards him and, as they met, they threw their arms around each other.

When they parted, Kevin looked at Chipper and said, "You found her!"

"It's not Pepper," Jeff said. "Look, the white spots are in different places."

Kevin was crestfallen. "Then who's this?"

"This is Chipper. Listen, what's happened to Pepper?"

Kevin instantly began to cry.

"She's been gone for a whole day now! We don't know what happened. We never let her out on her own. We always have her on the leash. But somehow she got out of the house! The front door must not have been latched or something!"

"But even if she got out, why wouldn't she come home?" Jeff asked.

"I don't know! That's why I'm putting up these flyers. Maybe someone has seen her." Kevin glanced down at Chipper again. "I thought your aunt wouldn't let you have a dog."

Jeff shrugged. "It's a long story." He reached out for the flyers in Kevin's hand. "Let me help you put these up. Get another staple gun or some tape and I'll do half. We can do the whole neighbourhood."

"Okay, give me—"

"Jeff."

Jeff spun around. Harry was standing there, a grim expression on his face.

"What is it, Harry?"

"You know this guy?" Kevin asked.

"Jeff, we need to get out of here," Harry said.

"What are you talking about?"

Harry paused. "It's not safe."

16

"What do you mean, it's not safe?" Jeff asked. He looked around. "I don't see anything that's not safe."

Harry pulled him in closer so that Kevin couldn't hear their conversation. "Don't you see what's going on?"

"What?"

"They've got your dog."

Jeff's jaw dropped. "You don't know that for sure."

"I'd bet anything The Institute has got Pepper."

Jeff felt a buzz from the phone he had in his hand. He glanced down at it.

I think so too.

Jeff looked at Chipper.

"You do?"

The dog nodded.

It makes sense.

"How does it make sense?"

Kevin, watching from a few feet away, said, "Uh, are you talking to your *dog*?"

89

Harry looked warily at Kevin, then turned back to Jeff and said, "Get in the van."

Jeff hesitated, then said to his friend, "Sorry, I gotta go."

"What's going on?" Kevin asked. "Who's this guy? Why are you talking to a dog? What does this have to do with Pepper? Are you in trouble? Jeff, come on, what's happening?"

Jeff gave his friend one last look and a shrug of hopelessness, then got into the van with Chipper.

As Harry started up the engine, his cell phone slipped out of the front pocket of his jeans and landed on the floor. There was so much going on that the man did not notice.

Chipper did.

He stared at it while Harry put the clunky old van's transmission into Drive and took off up the street, Kevin watching as they turned the corner.

Chipper kept his eye on Jeff, waiting until he was looking down into his lap, where he would instantly see a message from him the second he sent it.

Do not say anything.

Jeff's eyebrows rose a notch.

Harry's phone fell out of his pocket.

Jeff very slowly turned his head to look down towards the floor. His eyes fixed on the phone.

Pretend to drop your phone and pick up his. Then check recent texts and call history.

Jeff's head went up and down very slowly. A nod that only Chipper would notice. He needed to wait for the right time.

"Where are we going?" he asked Harry.

"We just need to get out of here," Harry replied. "If The Institute was in the neighbourhood, and if they grabbed Pepper, then they could still be hanging around looking for us."

"Why would they take Pepper?" Jeff asked.

Harry glanced his way. "Seriously?"

"Yes."

"They're trying to draw us out. They figured sooner or later we'd hear that Pepper was missing and put the facts together. Then they'll expect us to get in touch, see what they want. And what they're going to want is to make a trade."

"A trade?"

Harry tipped his head in Chipper's direction. "Chipper for Pepper." Harry kept glancing in his rear-view mirror. "I want to make sure no one is following us."

"Could they have put any tracking device on the van?"

Harry shook his head. "We only just got this one. I don't see how they could know. But like I said, if they saw us driving around here, they could be following. Hang on, I gotta pass this slowpoke."

Harry stomped on the gas, turned hard left, then right, as he passed an elderly driver wearing a baseball cap.

"They're always wearing hats!" he shouted. "Old guys in hats! Slowest drivers on the road."

When he made the sharp right, Jeff allowed his cell phone to fall out of his hands and hit the floor between the seats.

"Oops!" he shouted.

Harry kept his eyes on the road as Jeff bent over. He got his fingers around not only his own phone, but the one that had fallen out of Harry's pocket. Jeff sat back up in his seat, slid his own phone into his back pocket and clutched Harry's as if it were his. Angling the screen away from Harry's field of vision, he brought it to life and found it was already set to the texting function.

It was all Jeff could do not to gasp.

The last message Harry had sent said: **Are you ready? Can't keep driving around. It's time to deliver them to you.**

Who was Harry talking to? At the top of the screen it said: **Q**.

That was it. One letter.

Who was Q?

What was Q?

It sure didn't sound like a person. It sounded more like an organisation. But not The Institute. Or maybe it was another country. It could be anything!

So Chipper and he were right, Jeff thought. Harry had been up to something all along. He really *had*

92

been at Flo's Cabins solely to keep an eye on Jeff in case Chipper ever showed up!

Harry Green had pretended to be Jeff's friend, had gained his trust. And when Daggert and those other bad people from The Institute tracked Chipper down to his aunt's place, Harry had put his plan into action. He spirited Jeff and Chipper away, waiting for just the right time to hand them over to somebody else.

But was Q as bad as The Institute? Could he, or she, or it, be even worse?

Jeff feared it wasn't going to be long before he and Chipper found out.

Harry said, "Once I get us back out of the city I'll figure out where we go next. Don't you worry, everything's going to be okay."

Yeah, right, Jeff thought. *Once you've sold us out and been paid off, you'll be on your way.*

How was he going to tell Chipper what he now knew? While Chipper communicated with him through a texting function, Jeff just talked to him. Out loud. And anything he had to say now he sure did not want Harry to hear.

What Jeff needed to do was switch back to the other phone to see if Chipper had sent him any messages.

While Harry kept his eyes on the road, Jeff moved the man's phone to his back pocket and brought his own out. Casually, he looked at the screen.

Is it bad?

Jeff nodded ever so slightly.

Are we in trouble?

Another nod.

Do you think we need to make a run for it?

Yet another nod.

When I bark we run. Hold the door open for me.

Jeff nodded one final time and waited for the signal.

17

Once Daggert and Timothy had finished lunch, and brought a burger and fries out to the black van for Barbara, Timothy asked, "Should we have brought some food for the other one?"

"Not much point," Daggert said. "She needs to go down for a nap."

He was referring, of course, to Pepper, who was locked into a cage on the floor in the back of the van, still barking. Barbara was looking at her with great annoyance. Daggert knew he'd go mad if he had to listen to that all the time, so he said to Barbara, "Do you think you can get close enough to that mutt to lick her nose and use your sleepy slobber to knock her out?"

"I don't think so," Barbara replied.

That prompted Daggert to open a metal case next to his seat and take out some pellets that looked like doggie treats.

"Barbara, do not eat this, but give it to your new friend."

95

"Okay."

Barbara gingerly took the treat between her teeth, walked over to the cage and dropped the snack between the bars. Pepper snatched it up immediately, gave it a couple of quick chews, and swallowed.

"What a dummy," Barbara said in Daggert's ear.

It didn't take more than three minutes for Pepper to start yawning. By the time four minutes had gone by, she had curled up in the bottom of the cage and was fast asleep.

"She won't die, right?" Timothy asked.

The question, coming from Timothy, surprised Daggert. Maybe the kid had more of a capacity to feel sorry for other creatures than he'd first thought.

Daggert said, "She'll be asleep for quite some time."

Timothy smiled. "It was a good idea of mine, wasn't it, to grab the dog?"

Daggert reluctantly agreed. "Yeah, you're full of good ideas."

It had been incredibly easy. Once they'd found the house where Pepper lived, Timothy went up to the front door. He didn't knock, but he did try the door to see whether it was locked. When he found it was, he looked up and down the street in case anyone was watching. No one was. So he pulled out from his pocket a tiny set of tools that he used to pick the lock.

Given that Timothy had the skills, Daggert had agreed it was better for him to do it. A man bending over and fiddling with the lock was far more likely to attract attention.

Timothy had the door open in fifteen seconds. He turned the knob and let the door drift open about six inches. Then he walked back down to the sidewalk. Very soon, Pepper discovered the open door and, without a moment's thought, she decided to sample some freedom. She pushed open the door, padded down the steps, and sniffed the kerb.

Timothy said, "Hey there, girl! How you doing?"

Pepper wagged her tail and approached the boy. He scratched her head and ran his hand along her back.

The van slowly pulled up the street.

"Who's a good dog? Are you a good dog? I think you're a good dog."

Pepper wagged her tail even harder, and did not notice when Timothy looped his fingers around her collar.

The van was alongside them now. Daggert pushed a button and the side door slowly slid open.

"Come on, girl," said Timothy. "Let's go for a ride."

He pulled on Pepper's collar and led her right in. The second the two of them were inside, Daggert hit the button to close the door.

It was, Daggert thought, the easiest kidnapping in history.

The next one might prove more difficult.

Once they'd had lunch and given Barbara hers, they headed out of the city. They had a long drive ahead of them.

Daggert was curious about the time between Timothy's mother giving him up, and when he started being converted by The Institute. This was an aspect of his employer's work that did not know much about.

"So, when you were with this other agency, the one that got you from the adoption place, what was that like?"

Timothy said, "It was nice."

"Did you go to school?"

"There was a school there."

"Right. But was it fun?"

"I guess so," he said. "I remember playing games with the other kids, and there were lots of toys. Like video games and action figures. Stuff like that. But I don't need those things any more."

"What do you mean?"

"Well," said Timothy, "when you've been prepared to go out into the field, to do missions, you don't worry about having fun."

Daggert glanced over at the boy. "How do you feel about that?"

"I guess if my programming let me be sad, I would be," Timothy said. "But maybe it's a good thing not to have to worry about being sad."

Barbara watched their conversation intently.

"I never really thought about that," Daggert said.

Timothy nodded. "But I am capable of worrying. I worry it will make Madam Director unhappy if I'm not perfect."

"We all worry about that," Daggert said.

"Sometimes I dream about playing with toys."

"What were your favourite ones before . . . you know . . . before they made you into what you are now?"

"Trains," Timothy replied. "I loved trains."

"Really? I always liked trains, too." Daggert became uncharacteristically wistful. "When I was your age, my dad made me a train set. I used to run that little steam engine and four cars around the track all day."

Timothy gave him something that almost looked like a smile. "I bet that was fun."

Daggert thought back to those days. "It was. What else did you like to do?"

"I liked to draw. Especially spaceships. I can still draw, but I don't do it for fun. If I see something I failed to record, I can reproduce it later by hand."

Daggert smiled. "I used to sketch the Starship Enterprise when I was your age."

"What's that?"

"It's a spaceship from a TV show called *Star Trek*."

"Oh," Timothy said, nodding. "Were you any good?"

99

Daggert shrugged. "Not bad. What happens when you get older? Like, when you're ten, or fifteen, or even twenty?"

"I don't think much about that," Timothy said.

Daggert took another quick look at this child who seemed to exist only to serve the purposes of The Institute. He'd heard about kids being put to work early in some cultures, but this was something else altogether.

They drove on for a while longer without saying anything. Barbara was quiet, and Pepper remained asleep.

Finally, a sign up ahead caught Daggert's eye.
CANFIELD.

"We're almost there," Daggert said. "We go through this town. It's on the other side."

"Does this bring back memories?" Timothy asked.

Was the kid being sarcastic? Did Timothy know that the last time Daggert was here, things had gone horribly wrong for him and his team? Or was he just trying to be nice?

"Are you trying to be a wise guy?" Daggert asked.

Timothy gave him a puzzled look. "What do you mean?"

"Never mind," Daggert said. He drove through the small town, then out the other side. "We're almost there," he said. "Yep, up ahead, see that?"

Timothy and Barbara both looked out the front window and saw a sign that read:

SHADY ACRES
STRAIGHT AHEAD

Shady Acres, of course, was the camp Emily Winslow and her ex-cop father, John, ran.

Daggert said, "I must admit, this was a pretty good idea, Timothy. Once Jeff Conroy knows we've got his old dog *and* his little girlfriend, there's no way he won't give up Chipper."

18

Harry Green was talking as he drove.

"So, here's what I'm thinking. We're going to go to the media. We're going to go to one of the big networks, maybe CNN. We just show up and tell them our story — well, your story, this really doesn't have much to do with me — and once all of this goes public, then what's The Institute going to do? Huh? What *can* they do? There's no point going after Chipper here any more, or you, or doing anything to Pepper. What do you think about that?"

Jeff glanced down at the phone. His phone, not Harry's.

He is lying.

"Or maybe the *New York Times*? What do you think, Jeff? And what do you think, Chipper?"

"That might be a good idea," said Jeff. "But where are those places? I mean, I guess the *New York Times* is in New York, but what about CNN?"

"Maybe what we do," Harry said, "is we don't worry about finding out where they are. We get them to come to us. We find a safe place, we put in a call to their tip line or whatever it is, and wait for them to come and interview us. Once they meet Chipper here, and find out what he can do, believe me, they'll be convinced that something's up."

"What if someone listens in on that call?" Jeff said. "And gets to where we are before the reporters do?"

"Hmm," said Harry. "Let me think on that."

"And what if The Institute has people working secretly in any of these news organisations? What then?"

Harry gave Jeff an admiring look. "You don't want to trust anyone, do you?"

"I'm starting to think I can't," Jeff said.

The van was getting into heavy traffic. While they were several miles from the street where Jeff had once lived, they were still in the city. Harry, who'd been checking his rear-view mirror every few seconds, was confident no one was following them, and had started to relax a little.

"So, Harry," Jeff said, slowly, "what made you decide to rent a cabin at my aunt's place?"

"Huh?"

"Why her place, when you could have picked any other place that rented cabins?"

No!

"Why not?" Harry said. "Somebody told me it was a nice spot."

Do not ask questions like this! Harry will get suspicious.

Jeff turned his phone over so he wouldn't see Chipper's thoughts. It was time to get to the bottom of this, he figured. Before he and Chipper bailed out of this van, he wanted a better idea of what was going on with Harry Green.

Jeff wanted some answers.

"Who recommended the place to you?" he asked.

Harry shrugged. "I can't even remember off the top of my head. Must have been someone I worked with before I retired."

"So you didn't go there because you knew I was living there."

Harry gave his head a shake. "What? What are you talking about?"

Chipper was up on his hind legs, staring out the window. They were in a business district, with lots of buildings separated by narrow alleyways.

He liked the look of this.

"So you didn't book a cabin there to keep an eye on me, just in case Chipper ever showed up?"

"That is – what are you talking about?" Harry said, looking surprised.

"Who are you *really*?"

"I'm Harry Green!"

"Harry Green, with a backpack full of disguises

– why did you decide to help me in the first place? What was in it for you?"

Chipper felt this had gone on long enough. The van had stopped at a traffic light. This was as good a time as any.

He barked.

Loudly.

Jeff glanced at him, realised this was the signal, and threw open the passenger door.

"Hey!" Harry shouted. "What are you doing?"

Jeff leapt out, grabbing his phone and stuffing it into his front pocket. Chipper followed right on his heels, jumping over the empty passenger seat and landing on the street.

"No, no, no, no!" screamed Harry.

Jeff reached into his back pocket, found Harry's phone, and pitched it down the street. Without bothering to close the van door, he and Chipper ran. Chipper took the lead. In seconds, the boy and dog were gone.

Harry jumped out of the van. The light had changed to green and cars ahead of the van were starting to move. Horns began to blare from those stuck behind him.

"Come back!" he shouted. "Come back!"

But he'd already lost track of where they'd gone.

"Stupid, stupid, stupid!" he shouted to himself.

He ran down the sidewalk, his head moving rapidly from side to side, scanning for the phone Jeff had tossed. He spotted it on the ground next to a trash bin. He snatched it up and looked at the screen, worried that it might be cracked.

He pressed the button on the bottom of the phone and breathed a sigh of relief when it came to life. He opened up the contacts, found Q, and pressed. He didn't want to text. He wanted to talk.

"Come on, come on, pick up," he said, horns continuing to blare around him.

And then, someone answered.

"Yes?"

"It's me."

"You sound out of breath," the person on the other end of the call said. "What's happened?"

"They got away. Jeff and the dog are gone."

"What?"

"I'm sorry. Jeff was starting to get suspicious. He and the dog worked something out, a signal. They bolted from the van when I was stuck in traffic."

"You have to find them!"

"I know! But I need help."

There was a pause. "Okay, we'll meet you. We'll figure out what to do."

"It's all my fault," Harry Green said. "Please tell Patricia I'm so sorry, Edwin."

Edwin ended the call and turned to Patricia. He almost couldn't get the words out.

"He lost them," he said.

Patricia was horrified at first, then angry. "How? How did he lose them? How could he be so stupid?"

"He says Jeff and Chipper were on to him. They knew there was something fishy going on. And they took off."

"Then he should have just told them! He should have told them he was taking him to see us!"

"Patsy, we talked about this. We talked about this a hundred times. It was way too risky for Harry to tell Jeff we're alive. He might have thought it was a trick. And not only that, what if Harry went and got his hopes up, and then The Institute found us before we were all able to get back together!"

Patricia walked out of the cabin they had been living in for months, stood on the porch and crossed her arms angrily. The beautiful forest that surrounded their secluded home and the sounds of chirping birds did nothing to calm her.

Edwin joined her and put an arm around her shoulders, but she turned away.

"Jeff's going to be okay," he said. "As long as he has Chipper with him, he'll be okay."

"You don't know that," Jeff's mother said. "This entire year, whenever I think maybe we can relax, drop our guard, we're suddenly reminded just how much at risk we are."

Edwin didn't know what to say. Patricia was right, of course. Even after the plane explosion, their lives were constantly under threat.

They'd been steps away from the jet's open door when Edwin had decided he had to trust his wife's instincts, that it *was* Daggert she'd seen walking from the plane back to the gate. That could only mean bad news. At the very least, it meant he and Patricia were being watched. It had seemed very likely to Edwin that Daggert had placed other agents from The Institute on the plane to keep an eye on them.

About ten feet from the jet's door was another one that led from the jetbridge to a set of metal steps going down to the tarmac. Baggage handlers used this door to drop off checked bags for passengers when they were leaving the plane.

"This way," Edwin had said suddenly, grabbing his wife by the arm and steering her towards the door.

His timing was perfect. There was no one walking down from the gate at that time, and the flight attendant at the door to the jet had not been looking in their direction.

Edwin grabbed Patricia's bag and told her to get down the stairs as quickly as possible. It was night, and when they reached the tarmac, they felt they could make it to the terminal without being noticed. The trick would be finding an unlocked door allowing them back into the building.

While they watched, their plane backed away from the gate and moved out to the runway. Edwin glanced back and saw the plane accelerate, lift off and sail off into the night sky. He watched the pinpricks of red light from the plane's wings as it flew out over the water.

And then came the explosion. There was a huge ball of flame in the night sky, then trails of fire, like fireworks, heading towards the ground.

"Patsy!" he cried, holding her tight with one arm and pointing with the other.

"That's not—"

"That's our plane," he said. "That *was* our plane."

It only took seconds for them to realise the significance of what had just happened. They were supposed to be on that aircraft. If they'd taken their seats on that flight, they would now be dead.

Daggert.

"You don't think . . ." Patricia started to say.

Edwin nodded slowly. "The Institute wanted us dead. They thought if they took out an entire plane, no one would realise the only ones they wanted dead were us."

"That's . . . it's inhuman," Patricia said. And then she whispered, "Jeff."

Her whisper grew into something much louder. "What about Jeff? We have to get him! We have to get him right now!"

"No!" Edwin said. "No . . . let me think."

"What is there to think about?" she asked. "We have to get him immediately!"

"Patsy, listen!" Edwin said. "If they think we're alive, if they realise we were not on that flight, they're going to keep coming after us. And if we have Jeff with us, his life is in as much danger as ours!"

Patricia composed herself, and took a moment to think about what Edwin had said.

"You're right," she said. "But now what? What do we do?"

"The first thing we have to do is get out of here." He headed towards another door, hoping it might be unlocked, but Patricia pulled him back.

"No," she warned. "We'll get picked up on security cameras if we go that way. If we want The Institute to think they killed us, we can't be seen on surveillance after that plane blew up." She drew a long breath. "We have to go that way."

110

She pointed out to the runways, and what lay beyond.

"Do we bring the bags?" Edwin asked. But he realised it was a stupid question the moment he uttered it. Leaving the bags behind would be evidence they'd not boarded the plane. On top of that, they were going to need a few things while they figured out what they were going to do.

What they did was cross the runways, get through a fence, steal a car that had been left running while a man ran into a doughnut shop, and head as far away as they could, as fast as they could.

Along the way, they discussed Jeff's fate.

Of course, their son would be devastated to learn his mother and father had perished in a disaster. As horrible as that was, it was better than bringing him along. And there were already provisions in their will – Jeff's parents were careful to make plans for the future but had never imagined anything like this! He would go to live with Edwin's sister, Flo, who ran a fishing camp.

Jeff, they concluded, would be okay. Horribly, horribly distressed, but at least he would be safe from Madam Director and The Institute.

They decided they needed to find a hideaway, and there were several. Cheap motels, hostels, then, finally, this cabin in the woods. (They couldn't exactly rent one of Flo's.)

111

But they never stopped worrying.

What if The Institute ever figured out they were alive? What if the recovery efforts after the plane crash failed to turn up any evidence of them? That was when Edwin decided to get in touch with an old friend.

Harry Green.

Except his name was not Harry Green.

Long before Edwin Conroy had come to work at The Institute, he had been doing research for a NASA-related firm in Texas. The head of security there had been a kindly older man named Harvey Gaynor. But that kindness hid a tough inner strength. Although Harvey didn't talk about it, Edwin sensed the man had a secret past that might have involved working for the CIA or some other spy agency.

Whenever Edwin asked him about it, Harvey would smile and say, "Some things are off limits, my friend."

In fact, they became very good friends. Harvey retired around the time Edwin and Patricia were hired by The Institute.

"If you ever need anything," Harvey had told them, "you just ask."

So Edwin had found a way to get in touch with Harvey and told him he was worried about Jeff. If The Institute suspected Edwin and Patricia were alive, they could grab Jeff as a way of making them come out into the open.

"I can keep an eye on him," Harvey said. "My wife has passed away, I'm sitting around with nothing to do. Maybe it's time to do some fishing."

So Harvey booked one of Flo's Cabins for the summer.

When Chipper escaped, and found his way to Jeff – piecing together the things Jeff's parents had said to the dog as they transformed him into one of the smartest mutts in the world – Harvey had to step in and rescue the boy.

And the dog.

Harvey had been calling Edwin and Patricia with updates. When they all thought it was safe, they were going to arrange a reunion.

Everyone now believed the time had come.

But there was a problem.

Jeff and Chipper were gone. Harvey and Edwin and Patricia had to find them before The Institute did.

20

Jeff and Chipper raced down one alley, came out on to another city street, dodged slow-moving cars as they crossed it and disappeared down another alley, glancing back all the time in case somehow Harry was behind them.

They huddled by a loading dock at the back of a building to catch their breath. Jeff was doubled over, hands on his knees. Chipper's sides ballooned and collapsed, ballooned and collapsed. His tongue dangled from his jaws.

"I . . . I think we lost him," Jeff said. He glanced at the phone that was always in his hand.

Why did you throw away Harry's phone? It might have had information in it we could have used.

Jeff looked like he'd just missed the easiest question on a math test. "Oops. I was just trying to keep him from calling whoever he works for."

Chipper nodded his understanding, and appeared

ready to say something else, when suddenly he stopped breathing. He froze. He had his eyes on something. Jeff noticed and became instantly alarmed. The dog was looking in the direction of a fence that was lined with litter.

"What is it, boy?" Jeff asked, standing up and glancing at the phone that was always in his hand. "What do you see?"

When Chipper did not respond, he followed the dog's gaze. Jeff didn't see anything. Was the dog zeroing in on something on the other side of the fence? Jeff was pretty sure Chipper did not have X-ray vision. His high-tech eyeballs could be used as cameras, but they could not see through fences and walls, could they?

Suddenly, Chipper sprang. He bolted for the fence like a low-flying missile.

Oh no, Jeff thought. *What is it?*

Jeff didn't know whether to stay where he was, run after Chipper, or take off in the other direction. If Chipper was attacking some perceived threat, was Jeff going to put himself in danger by following? But then again, if Chipper was headed for trouble, he might need Jeff's help.

I'm going after him, Jeff thought. *I've got your back, Chipper. I'm right . . .*

But then he saw what Chipper was after.

A rat.

It came scurrying out from between two garbage cans. Chipper tore after the rat, but lost it when it disappeared between two more bins further down the alley. The dog became increasingly frantic as he stuck his snout into the narrow opening.

"Chipper!" Jeff shouted.

The dog stopped, froze, then turned his head around to look at the boy. Jeff looked at his phone.

Sorry.

"What is wrong with you?"

Chipper came trotting back, but not without looking back twice to see if the rat had reared its head, or shown off its long, slinky tail.

I am sorry. Now you see why The Institute wanted to put me down.

Jeff's anger immediately faded. He knelt down and took the dog into his arms then pulled him in close, their faces pressed together.

"It's okay," Jeff said. "How can I be mad at you for doing what a dog wants to do?"

Chipper did not respond.

"What? What are you thinking?"

I would like to be like other dogs.

"Don't say that. You're amazing the way you are."

Someday, when we are safe, would you promise to do something for me?

Jeff said, "Sure, I guess. What?"

Would you deactivate all my programming?

"What . . . do you mean?"

Turn off all my special features. You could not remove them from me. That might kill me. But I could tell you how to disconnect everything.

"But . . . but if I did that, what would happen?"

I would be like any other dog. Like Pepper.

Jeff frowned. "But . . . but we wouldn't be able to talk to each other the way we do now."

You loved Pepper even though you could not talk to her.

Jeff felt a lump growing in his throat. "Yeah, but that's different. She never could talk. But even if I did disconnect all that stuff, you'd still remember all we'd been through, right? I mean, you'd understand things in a way no other dog could."

No. I would be a dog. I want to chase rats and squirrels and rabbits and play catch and roll around in dead things like all the other dogs.

Jeff started to cry.

Please do not cry. You would not love me if I were like Pepper?

"Of course I would!" Jeff shook his head. "I don't want to talk about this any more."

Okay.

"I don't!"

I said okay.

117

Jeff cried a moment longer, then dug into his pocket in search of a tissue. He blew his nose, and dabbed his eyes.

"I'm okay now. But I don't want to lose you. Not only that, you've got me thinking about Pepper again. What are we going to do? If Daggert's got her, how will we get her back?"

I do not know.

"Come on!" Jeff said. "You've still got all your software. You're still this genius dog."

I do not have an idea that would not put you in danger. And right now we have a more urgent problem.

"What?"

We have escaped from Harry. But he could be looking for us. He might have called others to help hunt for us. We have no money. We have no one we can call for help.

"Yeah, well, when you put it like that, it is kind of a big problem." Jeff tried to blink the tears out of his eyes. "A minute ago you made me sad. Now you've scared me half to death. Things couldn't get a whole lot worse, could they?"

21

Emily Winslow had been feeling very worried, and very unhappy.

The thirteen-year-old girl hadn't had much time to get to know Jeff Conroy from the nearby Flo's Cabins, and she'd had even less time to get to know Chipper, but she missed them, and could not stop thinking about whether they were safe. She wished somehow Jeff could send a message to let her know he and Chipper were okay, but understood he'd be taking a risk to do it.

Emily's father still believed it was possible their own calls and emails were being monitored. And Emily was still disappointed in him, that he wasn't doing something – anything – to help Jeff and Chipper.

"Doesn't involve us," he'd told her more than once.

Emily had been feeling badly about the things she had said to her father the night before. She knew, in her heart, that his real concern was for her. She'd been trying to be extra nice today, and had made tuna sandwiches for lunch, which her dad really liked.

As he downed his last bite, John dabbed the corners of his mouth with his napkin and asked, "After we clean up, can you help me fix one of the docks? There's a plank on it that's gonna give way soon and I don't want any of our guests on it when it goes. That'd be a lawsuit for sure."

"Okay," she said.

As always, they did the dishes together, bumping shoulders. Anything that didn't go into the dishwasher John did by hand and passed to Emily to dry. Her father had always pledged to keep the house as neat and tidy as it had been when Emily's mother had been alive. Being in the police, Emily figured, was a little like being in the army. You learned that there was a place for everything, and everything had to be in its place. John liked things to be in order.

When they were finished, they went first to the shed, where John had a well-equipped workshop, to gather up what they would need. Saw, hammer, nails. Then they walked down to the water's edge and out on to one of the wooden docks.

"Watch your step," John said. "This is the one."

He tapped his foot on the plank. Then he applied some weight, and showed Emily how the board bent. "It's gonna snap right there. Someone steps on that, their leg goes through, they'll cut up their calf real good."

Emily nodded. She was carrying a plank about four feet long, although the one they were replacing was no more than three feet.

"Got the measuring tape?" John asked.

Emily had been holding it.

"Okay, you measure up the old board, then mark that length on the new one."

Emily got on her knees and ran the tape along the board. "It's thirty-five inches," she said. "Why couldn't I just lie the new board on the old one and take the measurement right off it? Just mark it with a pencil. What do I need a measuring tape for, anyway?"

John looked at her. "You're just like your mother."

"What does that mean?"

He smiled. "You make me look stupid on frequent occasions. Yeah, do it your way."

So Emily did just that. Once she had the new board marked with a pencil line, she handed it to her father. He hung the end of the board over the edge of the dock, got his knee on it, and picked up his handsaw.

"Can I saw?" Emily asked.

John stopped. "Sure."

She moved into the position he'd been in. She touched the teeth of the saw to the edge of the board.

"Let the weight of the saw do the work," he said. "Don't push down hard. It'll just jam."

Emily nodded and started sawing.

"Good," her father said. "Perfect."

She stopped halfway through the cut.

"Is it stuck?" he asked.

"No," Emily said. "I just wanted to apologise."

"Huh? Apologise for what?"

"For thinking bad things about you."

Her dad said nothing.

Emily said, "I'd been wondering if you'd changed. If maybe now you were scared of the bad guys. But I know that's not true. I know you just want to keep me safe. That's all I wanted to say."

She went back to sawing the board. In two minutes, she was through it. The end fell off into the water, but floated on top. She reached down, plucked it out and flung it on to the shore.

When she stood up her father put his arms around her. He held her like that for several seconds, saying nothing, then looked down at the board that was about to break and said, "I forgot the crowbar. That thing is really nailed in there."

As he let go of Emily, she said, "I'll go back to the shed and get it." She was glad of an excuse to slip away. She didn't want her father to see her cry.

"Okay," said her dad, who also seemed on the verge of tears.

Emily ran off the dock and out of sight.

As John stood on the dock, a fisherman he knew putted by in his small, aluminium boat.

"How's it going there, John?" the man called out.

John nodded and waved. "Good, good. You catching anything?"

The man reached over the side of the boat to a dangling chain – what was called a stringer – and lifted it out. There were four fish hooked to it.

"Wow!" John said. "That'll be some good eatin'."

"How about I give one of them to you and your girl for your dinner tonight?"

"I can't say no to that," John said. "Throw it in a skillet with some potatoes, it'll be heaven on a plate."

The fisherman's boat glided away. For someone who ran a fishing camp, John did not get out in a boat with a pole and bait very often. There was always work to do around Shady Acres.

At least he had the winters to recharge. The fishing camp closed in October, about six weeks from now, and did not reopen until the following May. If Emily weren't in school, it would have been nice to go someplace for a month, or even a few weeks, for a vacation. France, maybe, or London. John had always wanted to take his daughter to Europe, show her the things he thought she needed to see. The Tower of London, the Louvre, Notre Dame Cathedral. He had some money saved up and figured it was time to spend some of it.

So long as he and Emily kept a low profile, showed no interest in what happened to Jeff and that robot dog of his, he figured they'd be okay.

He turned away from the lake and looked back to the shore.

Emily was taking a long time to find a crowbar.

John was pretty sure it was hanging in its usual place – on the wall just inside the door to the shed. He wondered if he could have used it somewhere and forgotten to put it back. That wasn't like him. He was pretty particular about his tools.

Slowly, he walked off the dock.

"Emily!" he shouted.

He picked up his pace as he headed for the shed. He called out his daughter's name again but there was no reply.

He reached the shed and poked his head in. The crowbar was hanging on the wall right where he'd put it.

"Emily!" he yelled again.

Maybe she'd gone into the house. Just a bathroom visit, he told himself. So he waited out front of the house for another half a minute, expecting her to come out any second.

She did not.

John stepped into the house and looked up the stairs.

"Emily!" he shouted. "Everything okay?"

There was no reply. John checked the kitchen, then bounded up the stairs to the second floor. He checked every room for Emily, but did not find her.

Maybe, he thought, she was back down by the water, waiting for him to return and fix the dock. He ran down the stairs, out the front door, and to the water's edge without stopping. His heart was pounding in his chest.

Emily was not at the dock.

He cupped his hands around his mouth, turning them into a megaphone. "Emily!" he cried.

Emily did not answer.

Emily was gone.

22

Chipper had an idea.

You know how to drive.

Jeff said, "Well, kinda. I drove Aunt Flo's old pickup truck. And for about five minutes, I drove Daggert's big honking SUV."

So if we find a car you can drive it and we can get away.

"I don't want to steal a car!" Jeff protested.

You would only be borrowing it.

"If we get a car, where are we going to go?"

Harry had that idea about going to a newspaper or TV news station. I do not think he really meant to do it but it is an idea.

"Right!" said Jeff. "But where would we go? I don't know anything about that kind of stuff. I never watch the news or anything."

Let me research that.

Chipper seemed to freeze for a moment as he searched his memory banks.

There are big papers in New York and Washington. New York is closer.

"Uh, you want me to drive into New York City?"

Is that a problem?

"For someone who's only ever driven from a fishing camp to a garbage dump on a country road, yeah, that's a problem."

I think you can do it.

"Just because you think so doesn't make it so. Can't we just take a train or something?"

They will be looking for us in train stations. Not safe. But I

Jeff was looking at the phone and wondered why Chipper had stopped in mid-thought.

"But you what?" he asked.

Chipper was no longer looking at him. His body had begun to tremble. His eyes, which weren't real eyes anyway, appeared more distant than normal, as if he was not focused on anything at all.

"What's going on with you?" Jeff said. "Are you okay?"

Chipper swayed. He appeared ready to fall over. Jeff knelt down and put his arms around the dog so he would not collapse, but turned his hand so he could still read his phone.

"Talk to me, Chipper. What's going on?"

Trying to make contact with

"What? Someone is trying to make contact with you?"

System invasion

"What's a system invasion? Someone is trying to invade your software? But Emily turned all that stuff off before we got away."

Jeff felt increasingly frightened. Something was very wrong with Chipper.

"Is it The Institute? Is it Daggert?"

Message. Trying to send a

"Who's trying to send a message?"

Now Chipper was trembling even more. It was just like what had happened to him on the gravel road near that dump, when Jeff first found him, nearly running him over with his aunt's truck.

"Are they trying to find us?" he asked.

Not find just messa

"Can't you shut them out? Can't you turn off whatever it is they're latching on to?"

Jeff could imagine what might be happening at The Institute. There was probably an entire team devoted to re-establishing contact with Chipper. If they could find a way to do it, they'd get word to Daggert.

Suddenly, Chipper went limp.

"Oh no, oh no," Jeff said, as Chipper slid through his arms to the ground. "Please don't be dead, please, please, please."

He placed his palm on the dog's chest and was pretty sure he could still feel it going up and down.

Jeff huddled over Chipper, held him tight, and whispered into his ear, "If you let them make contact, even for a second, will you be okay? Let them tell you what they have to tell you, then shut them down again? Can you do something like that? Even if it means they know where we are, for a second, then we can make a run for it. Huh? What about that? Is that a plan?"

Chipper's tail thumped. Once.

"Yes!" Jeff said. "That's it! You're going to be okay!"

Another thump. But this weak wag of the tail did not suggest that Chipper was happy. It was a signal to Jeff that he was listening, that he understood.

Chipper trembled for another second, then went very still.

Jeff released his hold, but stayed on his knees next to the dog as he slowly raised his head.

"You're okay, right?" Jeff asked, looking at his phone.

I think so.

"What was that all about? Who was sending a message?"

The Institute.

"Was it Daggert? Was it him?"

Chipper actually moved his head from side to side.

No. It was someone named Timothy.

"Timothy? Who the heck is Timothy?"

I do not know.

"What did he say?"

Pepper and Emily. The Institute says it has them both.

23

"Hey!" Emily shouted. "Hey! Mr Sunglasses!"

Daggert looked through his shades into the rear-view mirror of the almost windowless cargo van he was piloting. Why the manufacturers had installed a rear-view mirror when the van's back doors had no windows was baffling, but it allowed him to regularly glance at the cage holding Pepper and, now, Emily Winslow. The two of them were crammed in tightly together. While Pepper had enough room to stand, Emily had to sit, and even crouch over a little, to fit within the wire box.

"You can't do this to me!" she shouted. "This is against the law!"

Timothy, in the passenger seat, was fiddling around with a laptop, seemingly unbothered by the noise Emily was making. Barbara, as always, stood in the space between the seats, front paws up on the console so she could see the road ahead.

Daggert had the van cruising down the highway at seventy miles per hour. He was planning no further stops – not even a bathroom break, he'd warned Timothy and Barbara – until they returned to The Institute.

"You're going to be in big trouble for this!" Emily shouted. "My dad was a cop!"

Daggert looked over at Timothy, tapping away on the computer that sat on his lap.

"Don't you find her constant screaming a bit distracting?" Daggert asked the boy.

Timothy took his eyes off the screen long enough to catch Daggert's eye, then looked back at what he was doing. "No," he said. "I can focus."

"I *know* how to focus," Daggert said. The kid was kind of growing on him, but there were still times when Daggert found him annoying. Who wouldn't be annoyed by a six year old who was probably smarter than you?

"If her screaming bothers you, it's evidence you can't focus," Timothy said.

"Let me ask you something, *Timmy*," Daggert said. "Were you a know-it-all when you were still just a regular boy, or did it happen after Madam Director stuffed you full of circuits and software?"

Timothy regarded him thoughtfully. "I believe," he said, almost with a hint of sadness, "I was a nice boy."

"Oh," Daggert said.

"You don't think I'm nice now?"

"Well, it's not that. You just seem . . . very sure of yourself."

"I can't help it," Timothy said. "They've filled my head with so much data that it's hard to hold back."

Daggert almost grinned. "Sort of like me. I can't help being this handsome." Timothy stared at him blankly. "It's a joke."

"Oh," Timothy said. "A grown-up sense of humour is something I still have to work on."

"Hello?" Emily shouted. "Earth to nutbars?"

Daggert could not resist a glance in his mirror, but Timothy did not react at all. Instead, he pointed to his screen. "I was successful in sending a message."

"You were?"

"I linked through The Institute's computers and attempted to restore the hookup with H-1094, which, as you know, has disabled its ability to receive messages. But I was able to find a way to break through, however briefly, and send a short one."

"How did you do that?"

"It's a bit like pushing a really fat person through a small window. You push and push and finally – whoosh! – it goes through."

"When you sent that message, were you able to determine a location?"

"No," Timothy said, shaking his head.

"So you're not a complete genius, then."

"I might ask Barbara for help," Timothy said, patting the dog on top of her head.

"*I'm ready to help*," Barbara said in Daggert's ear.

"Is anyone listening to me?" Emily cried. "You can't do this to a person! You can't just kidnap a person and take them away!"

Well, as it turned out, they could.

* * *

Two hours earlier, Emily had run in the direction of the workshed to get her father a crowbar. But before she got there, she'd spotted a small boy playing with a beautiful Labrador retriever. The boy threw a stick and the dog raced after it.

Emily wondered who they were. She hadn't seen the boy or the dog at Shady Acres before, and the fishing camp she helped her father run was small enough that you got to know everyone who was there very quickly.

But it was possible these two had wandered into Shady Acres from one of the cabins down the lake, or even from Flo's Cabins. Plenty of people from up and down the lake wandered through the camp. Maybe, technically, it was trespassing, but it was also good for them to explore their fishing camp. One day, they might end up becoming customers.

"That's a pretty dog you have there," Emily said.

"Thanks!" said the boy.

The dog grabbed the stick and came running back to him. The boy wrestled the stick out of its mouth.

"What's his name?" Emily asked.

"*Her* name is Barbara," the boy said.

"Hey there, girl," Emily said.

The boy threw the stick again. He was only about five or six years old, Emily guessed, so he didn't have a very strong arm, and he couldn't throw the stick that far – not much more than thirty feet.

Barbara collected the stick within seconds.

"You wanna throw?" the boy asked.

"Sure," Emily said. Once the boy had the stick out of Barbara's mouth he handed it to Emily. She tried to grab it in a spot where it wasn't covered in dog slobber, but once she had thrown the stick – more than twice as far as the boy could pitch it – her hand was wet and sticky.

As she wiped her hand on her jeans she asked the boy, "What's your name?"

"Timothy," he said.

"Well, hello, Timothy. Do you have a cabin around here?"

He pointed north. "Up that way."

This time, when Barbara returned with the stick, she came to Emily, who dropped to her knees. She grabbed for the stick with one hand, and patted Barbara's head affectionately with her other. She ran her hand down Barbara's head towards her collar.

"You sure have a nice coat," Emily said.

Barbara gave Emily a huge lick on the face. Her thick, moist tongue ran over Emily's mouth and nose.

"Blecch!" she said, but in a funny way. She didn't want to offend Timothy or Barbara.

When her hand reached the collar, she noticed something funny about it. It was much thicker than most collars dogs wore.

She felt a small shiver run up her spine.

"Yessir, you are one nice dog," she said, attempting to remain calm as she ran her hand down Barbara's neck once again. This time, when she reached the collar, she tried to work her fingers between it and Barbara's fur.

She could not get her fingers in there. It was as though Barbara's collar were stitched right to her body.

Emily only knew one other dog with a collar like that.

She had a feeling that if she felt around a little more, she'd find a port where you could link this dog to a computer.

Emily stood, stick in hand.

Stay cool, she thought.

She was only a few steps from the shed, only a few steps from getting that crowbar for her father. She realised now she might need it for herself. The idea of hitting a dog with a crowbar did not appeal to her at all, but she felt she might soon find herself in a desperate situation.

Just because Chipper turned out to be a friendly dog from The Institute did not mean Barbara was going to be one. And what about Timothy? What was his story? Why would an ordinary kid be hanging out with a dog like this?

She was thinking that when she threw the stick, and Barbara went after it, she would make her move.

She hurled it forward with everything she had.

"Go get it, girl!"

Except Barbara did not run. She was watching Emily, as if waiting for something to happen. Little Timothy was watching her, too.

"What's going on?" Emily asked. "What are you looking at?"

Timothy said to Barbara. "Soon?"

Barbara's head went up and down.

"What's soon?" Emily asked.

And then she dropped to the ground. It was like fainting, but not like fainting. She felt herself falling very quickly asleep.

As she lay there, eyes almost shut, Timothy looked down at her and said, "Barbara has a few options Chipper doesn't. Soon as she licked your face, I knew you only had a minute or so."

Barbara used her mouth to grab Emily by the ankle and drag her back to the van.

* * *

When they got to the gates of The Institute, Daggert came to a stop and powered down the window. The guard immediately recognised him, and hit the button to swing the gates wide. Daggert drove around to the rear of the building and backed up to a loading dock. He, Timothy and Barbara got out and went around to the van's rear door. The loading dock door slowly rose to reveal a receiving area with gleaming white walls. Standing next to a small forklift was a woman in coveralls. Daggert spoke to her while Timothy opened up the van.

The woman started up the forklift and drove it to the back of the van, the forks on the front sliding under the cage that held Emily and Pepper. The forks rose a few inches, lifting the cage off the van floor.

"What are you doing?" Emily demanded, her fingers looped around the wires of the cage. Pepper barked with agitation. "Where are you taking us?"

No one answered. The forklift backed up, turned around, and headed for the back wall of the receiving area. A floor-to-ceiling panel, designed to look so much like the rest of the room as to be almost invisible, retracted into the wall, allowing the forklift to enter deeper into The Institute.

Emily's angry shouting and Pepper's frantic barking ceased to be heard as the panel slid back into place.

24

"What are you telling me?" Jeff asked Chipper. "The Institute's got Pepper and Emily?"

We do not know that.

"What do you mean? Isn't that the message you got?"

Yes. Just because it said that does not mean it is true. But given that Pepper is missing, that part is probably true.

"Well, how do we find out for sure?"

Chipper thought for a moment.

You should call John Winslow. Find out if Emily is with him.

Jeff blinked. "Yeah, okay, that makes sense. Except, I can't use this phone for anything but to talk to you. If I connect it to the network they could figure out where we are. And we don't have any money, so unless you can turn yourself into another phone and a cash machine, I don't know what we're going to do."

We need to go shopping.

"Uh, what?"

We need to go to a store. A big store.

Jeff slowly shook his head. "So, you want to buy a new flea collar or something? Some dog biscuits?"

There is no reason to be insulting. I do not have fleas. Where there are shoppers there will be handbags. It is easier to take a phone from a handbag than a man's pocket.

"Okay, so we're going to turn into criminals. We're going to steal someone's phone."

Is there anything you would not steal to save Emily and Pepper?

Chipper had him there. He told Jeff the rest of his plan. Jeff wasn't sure it was perfect, but given that it was the only plan they had, he thought it was worth a try.

Now they had to find a store.

They emerged from the alley on to a busy sidewalk. Chipper used his high-tech artificial eyes to scan for Harry Green.

I do not see him.

Jeff pointed up the street. "There's a big department store. What about there?"

Okay.

They ran the half-block to the store. The entrance was a set of revolving doors.

That looks very dangerous.

"You've never seen doors like that?"

No.

"Stay close to me," Jeff said. Once some customers had exited the store and the door had stopped revolving, he beckoned Chipper to follow him.

Chipper froze.

"Come on, boy."

Chipper stared at the door, studying how it operated. If you entered at the wrong moment, you'd be trapped! If someone from the other side then pushed on the door too hard, you could be cut in half!

I cannot do it.

"Are you kidding me?" Jeff said. "You're like the bravest, most amazing dog in the whole world and you're afraid of a revolving door?"

Give me a second.

"No, it's okay. Look, we can go in one of the other doors, or I can pick you up and carry you in."

Carry me?

"Yes."

Chipper imagined that. Jeff having to scoop him up in his arms. How humiliating would that be? No, he couldn't let that happen. He'd have to find another way in, or—

"Here we go!" Jeff said, quickly bending over and grabbing Chipper just under his front legs.

No!

But Jeff had tucked his phone away to be able to get both hands on Chipper and was unable to read the message. Chipper bucked and squirmed in Jeff's arms.

"Stop it!" Jeff shouted. "I'm just trying to help!"

But Chipper would not stop, and there was no way Jeff could take him into the spinning doors with him acting that way. So Jeff had to drop him back down to the sidewalk.

"Yikes," Jeff said. "We'll find another way in." He had his phone back in his hand.

No, wait.

"What now?" Jeff said, on the edge of completely losing his patience.

I have to do this.

Chipper stared at the door as people continued to enter and exit the store. He had to get the timing just right.

I will go in first.

"Fine," Jeff said, taking a step back towards the street. "Take your time. It's not like we have anything else to do. I mean, sure, Emily and Pepper have probably been kidnapped and who knows what The Institute is doing to them, but you take your time screwing up your courage to go through a—"

Chipper bolted.

He'd known he could get his body into the doors without a problem, but it was his tail he was worried about. What if that got caught, just as it had when he was fleeing that subway car just after he'd escaped The Institute? When you thought about it, a tail could be a real nuisance.

The other thing he had to figure into the equation was that he was not powerful enough to actually push the door. He had to depend on customers coming the other way to give the door some momentum.

It was a good thing he had a brain capable of calculating the precise moves he had to make.

Just at the right moment, he slipped into the doors like a fast-moving snake with legs. He kept his snout pressed to the glass door in front of him and his tail tucked close to his body. The moment the door opened on to the inside of the store he shot out.

Once Chipper was in the store he spun around and looked expectantly at Jeff, who had watched his performance with wonder. Jeff entered the doors, pushed his way through, and joined Chipper.

"Well done," Jeff said.

Nothing to it.

Jeff laughed. "Okay, so now—"

"Hold it right there!"

They both turned to see a store security guard eyeing them, arms crossed.

"Uh, yes?" said Jeff.

"You can't bring a dog into the store!" the man said.

Chipper thought, *Are you kidding me? After all that?*

"Um, we're only going to be here for a minute," Jeff said.

"It doesn't matter whether it's one minute or one hour!" the guard said. "Dogs can't come in here."

How dare a store have a policy that bans dogs? Chipper thought. He wanted to go over and pee on the guard's shoe, but knew that was probably not the best way to handle the situation.

"Here's the thing," Jeff said, improvising. "The dog is here . . . for an interview. Well, we both are, sort of."

The guard said, "What?"

"In fact, you should be nice to him, because you might be *working* with him."

"What are you talking about?"

"This is a very special dog who's been trained to catch shoplifters. Chipper, is anyone shoplifting?"

Chipper froze, then slowly moved his head to the right, looking up an aisle that sold jewellery. He moved in classic border collie fashion, one paw slowly moving ahead of the other as he proceeded up the aisle.

"What is he—"

"Shh," Jeff said to the guard. "He's on to someone."

The guard watched Chipper stealthily move further into the store.

"I never worked with no dog before," the guard said.

"Well, you'll be lucky if you get to work with this one," Jeff said. "He's among the best."

Chipper was edging closer to a woman who was leaning over a glass display case, examining watches. Her long-strapped handbag hung over her shoulder and all the way down to her thigh. It was unclasped.

The woman was so consumed with looking at the watches she did not notice Chipper sticking his nose into her bag.

"Whoa," said the security guard. "He found something?"

"Looks like it," Jeff said.

Chipper withdrew his snout from the bag. Clutched delicately in his jaws was a cell phone.

"She stole a phone?" the guard asked.

"The dog's not usually wrong about these things," Jeff said. "You sell those kinds of phones here?"

The guard nodded. "Up on the second floor," he said.

"Well," said Jeff. "There you go."

"I wonder if I should go and arrest her," the guard said.

"I think that's a good idea," Jeff said, as Chipper started walking back towards him and the guard.

Jeff took the phone from Chipper's mouth and shook his head, feigning disappointment. "It's awful when people think they can help themselves to things that aren't theirs."

"Tell me about it," the guard said. "Uh oh, looks like she's going to get away."

The woman who had been examining watches was heading towards an escalator near the centre of the building.

The guard called out, "Hey, you!" He started to run after the woman.

Jeff examined the phone, mentally crossing his fingers that it was not password-protected. He hit the button at the bottom and the screen came to life.

"Yes!" he said.

The guard had grabbed the woman by the elbow. She was shrieking at him as he pointed back at Jeff and the dog.

"Time to go," Jeff said. They both turned and looked at the revolving door, and considered the obstacle it presented to a hasty getaway.

Fine.

Jeff knelt down, got Chipper into his arms, and carried him into the revolving doors. In seconds, they were outside. Jeff set Chipper on to the sidewalk.

How embarrassing.

"Yeah, well, you'll get over it. Let's go and call Emily's dad."

25

While Emily and Pepper were being settled in a cell at The Institute, Daggert went to report to Madam Director.

"Well?" she said, as he entered her office.

"We have the boy's dog and his girlfriend. That should draw him and H-1094 out."

Madam Director nodded approvingly. "Good plan. Who came up with that?"

Daggert was going to lie and say it was his idea, but he knew Madam Director had a way of eventually getting to the truth. So he said, "My new partner."

"Timothy or Barbara?"

That hurt. So she was willing to believe that it could just as easily have been the dog.

"Timothy," he said.

"He's working out very well, wouldn't you say?"

"Yes," Daggert said, "but . . ."

"But what?"

"There's something about him. I can't quite put my finger on it."

"I don't understand what you mean," Madam Director said.

"There are moments, when you get past all the upgrades we've made to him, when you can see the original boy who's in there. There's something about . . . that."

"I still don't understand."

"Where did you find him?" Daggert asked. "What's his history? Who were his parents?"

"Why is that important?"

"I like to know who I'm working with."

"Would you like to know who Barbara's mommy and daddy were, too?" she asked, with a sneer.

"No, that . . . won't be necessary."

Madam Director leaned back in her leather chair and crossed her arms. "Daggert, on any issue, you only need to know what I think you need to know. I can tell you that Timothy came to us the way the other child operatives now in development came to us. Through proper channels. Adoption agencies. These are children who needed a home, and we have provided one for them. In return, they will help us with our mandate, which is to make this a safer world."

"Of course," he said, backing down. "Thank you." He turned to leave, then thought of one more thing. "Uh, is Watson still around?"

"Wilkins, you mean?"

"Yes, Wilkins."

"What makes you ask?" She smiled devilishly.

"Well, the last time I was here, Timothy told you what he heard Wilkins saying about you."

"And you wondered if I had terminated . . . his employment?"

"Something like that."

"Don't be silly. He's a valued member of The Institute."

"Good. I want to see if he's picked up anything on the girl's father's phone. Maybe the boy has tried to get in touch."

Madam Director nodded. "Off you go, then."

Daggert left the office and went to the adjoining control room, where he found Wilkins tapping away on a keyboard in front of his monitor.

"Wilkins," Daggert said.

Wilkins turned to look at him but said nothing. Daggert thought perhaps he was stunned that he'd remembered his name correctly.

"You getting anything off John Winslow's phone?" he asked.

Wilkins shook his head.

"How about when Timothy broke through briefly to the dog? Did that narrow down its location at all?"

Wilkins shook his head again.

"What's going on?" Daggert asked. "You don't want to talk to me?"

Wilkins shook his head a third time.

A woman sitting at another terminal about five feet away noticed Daggert's frustration and said, "He burned his tongue."

Daggert frowned. "Must be pretty bad if you can't talk. How'd you do it?"

Wilkins looked pleadingly at the woman so that she would offer a fuller explanation.

"Madam Director. At first she was going to make him gargle acid for what he said about her, but then she put his coffee in the microwave on high for five minutes and made him drink it right away. He'll probably be able to talk again in a few days."

This time, Wilkins nodded. His co-worker had gotten the story right.

"Oh," Daggert said. "Sorry about that."

Wilkins shrugged, as if to say, *What are you gonna do?*

Daggert leaned over to whisper in the man's ear. "Given how so much of what we say around here can be overheard, I'll say this quietly."

Wilkins' eyes went wide.

"I have a favour I want you to do for me."

Wilkins suddenly appeared very anxious.

"I want you to run a test on something." Daggert dug into his pocket and pulled out a clear plastic evidence bag that contained a single straw.

Wilkins looked curiously at the straw.

"You're going to find some milkshake on it," Daggert whispered. "But you're also going to find the DNA of the person who was drinking the milkshake. I want to know everything about that DNA. I want to know if there even is any DNA, because I'm not entirely sure this person isn't one hundred per cent robot. I know we have the capability to do that kind of analysis very, very quickly."

Wilkins opened his mouth, giving Daggert a glimpse of his burnt tongue. It looked like an overcooked steak. Wilkins struggled to say just one word.

"No."

"Yes," Daggert said, leaning in closer. "Because there's something going on, and it's just not right."

Daggert stared long and hard into Wilkins' eyes. It was more a pleading look than a threatening one.

Wilkins slowly nodded his head.

26

Before calling John Winslow, Chipper said they needed to take some precautions.

The Institute might be listening in to John's calls. So Jeff opened a browser on the stolen phone – he was feeling badly that they were not going to be able to return it very easily to the woman they'd taken it from – and found a number for the Jenkins family.

The Jenkinses raised chickens on a farm about a quarter of a mile from Flo's Cabins. Aunt Flo liked to buy her eggs from them, and often sent Jeff in her pickup truck over there for a dozen. Chipper did not think it was likely The Institute would have bugged the Jenkins' phone.

So Jeff called the number and got Andy Jenkins, the husband.

"Hi, Mr Jenkins. It's Jeff Conroy."

"Jeff!" said Andy. "Haven't seen you around lately! You buying your eggs at the supermarket now?"

"No, sir, we would never do that. Listen, this'll

sound really weird, but there's something I need you to do, and you can't ask why."

"What?"

But Andy did what he was asked, which was to drive down to Shady Acres, find John Winslow, and get him to come back to the Jenkins' farm to take a phone call. When John asked what was going on – as he was sure to do – Andy was to refuse to answer his questions. Oh, and Andy was to tell him to be quick about it. The call was coming in ten minutes.

When Jeff called the second time, the phone at the farm was picked up even before the end of the first ring.

John Winslow said, "Who is this?"

In just three words, Jeff could hear the panic in his voice. That pretty much answered his first question, which was going to be whether Emily was missing.

"It's me, Mr Winslow. It's Jeff."

"Jeff! This is all your fault!" His voice had gone from panicky to angry in a single second.

"Mr Winslow, please listen to—"

"Emily should never have gotten mixed up with you! I blame you!"

"I'm so sorry, Mr Winslow, but please, tell me what's—"

"I'll tell you what's happened! She's gone, that's what's happened! They've grabbed her! They've got Emily!"

"Yes, sir, we figured that was what had happened."

"We? Who's with you?"

"Chipper, sir. The dog."

"That's what this is all about, isn't it? It's about that stupid dog!"

"Sir, if he were a stupid dog, they wouldn't want him back. Have you called the police or—"

"I haven't been able to do anything! They phoned and said if I called the police or anyone else something terrible would happen to Emily." He paused for a second. "I don't know what to do . . . I have to get her back."

Now Emily's dad sounded like he was starting to cry.

Jeff took the opportunity to speak softly. He said, "Mr Winslow, I am very, very sorry. Believe me, I never wanted any of this to happen. If I had known that Emily was going to get into trouble, I never would have asked her to help Chipper. But there isn't anything I can do about that. But maybe, just maybe, if we work together, we can get Emily back. And Pepper."

"Pepper?" said Emily's dad. "Who is Pepper?"

Jeff told him. "The Institute has Emily and Pepper, and they're going to hang on to them until I give them Chipper."

"Well, then, it's simple. Give them that dog!"

Jeff looked into Chipper's eyes. Even though they weren't real eyes, he believed he could see something in them. Something of Chipper's soul. And even if Jeff was just imagining seeing it there, that didn't

154

mean Chipper didn't have one. He had a personality. Chipper had . . . what was the word Jeff was trying to think of? Chipper had a spirit. And if all his software were removed from him tomorrow, he'd still have that.

"I . . . I don't know that I can do that," Jeff said.

"If you don't, they'll kill your other dog, and my little girl."

"There has to be another way," Jeff said. "There has to be a way to save Emily, and Pepper, and Chipper." He paused. "But I can't do it alone. I'm going to need help. I'm going to need help from someone I can trust, and I think the only person I can trust right now is you."

"What about Harry Green?" John asked. "Where's he? Let me talk to him. Put him on the phone."

"Harry Green turned out not to be the friend I thought he was," Jeff said. "He was working behind our backs, telling someone he had Chipper and me. We had to get away. For all we know, he was working for The Institute, or maybe some foreign government. The whole reason he was staying at my aunt's place was in case Chipper showed up."

Jeff took a deep breath.

"Mr Winslow, one way or another Chipper and I are going to rescue Emily and Pepper. We have no money, we have no car, and I'm talking to you on a stolen phone. We'll find a way to rescue them in spite of all of that. But we might have a better chance if you helped us."

Emily's dad was quiet for several seconds.

"Where are you?" he asked, finally.

Jeff told him.

"I'm on my way."

27

John Winslow was not the only one jumping into a vehicle and racing to the city.

Edwin and Patricia Conroy were too. Patricia got behind the wheel of their small sedan and Edwin jumped in beside her. As they approached the city, Edwin phoned Harry.

"We're almost there," he said. "What can you tell us?"

"I don't have good news," Harry said. "I drove around, hoping I'd spot them, but no luck. Now I'm on foot, looking in stores and down alleys."

"It's a big city," Edwin said. "Too big for one man to search."

"If only there was some way to get a message to them – some way for *you* to get a message to him, that might bring them out of hiding."

"Where are you now?" Edwin asked.

Harry told him.

"I think we can be there in fifteen minutes."

Patricia glanced over at him. "Ten," she said, leaning harder on the accelerator.

Harry waited on the corner, watching for them. Patricia spotted him, steered the car to the kerb, killed the engine, and she and Edwin got out. Edwin and Harry shook hands, and Patricia gave their old friend a quick hug.

"Well?" she said. "Where do we start?"

"He's your boy," Harry said, "and you programmed that dog. What do you think they would do? They've got no money, no phone, no way out of here."

Edwin gave that some thought. "You said he's been driving, right?"

Harry nodded.

"They might have stolen a car to get out of town."

Harry said, "It's possible, but risky. There are a lot more police around here than on those dirt roads around Flo's Cabins. They'd spot a kid behind the wheel."

"Well, I'm pretty sure *Chipper* won't be driving," Edwin said. "We made it possible for him to do a lot of things, but not *that*."

"The good news is," Patricia said, "Chipper will do anything he can to protect Jeff."

"If Jeff hasn't gotten hold of a car," Harry said, shaking his head with a measure of defeat, "he might still be in the area." Harry pointed across the street. "They went into an alley in that block."

158

Edwin said, "If they got access into any of those buildings, found an empty apartment—"

"Enough talk!" Patricia said. 'Let's start searching." And with that, she looked both ways and crossed the street, heading for an alley.

"Let's go," Edwin said to Harry, and the two of them set off after her.

Once they'd caught up with Patricia, Harry suggested that they split up to cover ground more quickly. "You two head down this one," he said, pointing down the closest alley. "I'll go up to the next alley, then we'll meet around the back."

Edwin gave him a thumbs-up.

* * *

The stolen phone in Jeff's pocket rang. He and Chipper had been nestled between two garbage cans behind a four-storey apartment building, hiding until John Winslow got in touch.

Jeff jumped. "That must be him!" he cried.

The Chipper phone read: **Good!**

Jeff put the stolen phone to his ear and said, "Hello? Mr Winslow?"

"Who is this?" a woman said angrily. "Are you the one whose dog stole my phone? Because if I catch you and that mutt of yours, I'm going to— "

"I'm sorry!" Jeff said. "I'm sorry we stole it! We'll give it back, I promise!"

"I'm going to call the police!"

"We only need it for a little longer! Please, don't call the police!"

Hang up.

Jeff looked at Chipper.

John Winslow might call at any moment.

"I have to go," Jeff told the woman. "Really, honestly, we'll try to figure out how to get your phone back to you. And we're hardly using any data, so you don't—"

"I want my phone back right now!"

"Sorry," Jeff said. "I have to go." He ended the call and looked at Chipper. "She was super mad."

Before Chipper could respond, the phone rang a second time. Jeff jumped again. He looked at the screen and saw a different number to the one that had just called.

He put the phone to his ear, more tentatively this time.

"Hello?"

"Jeff?"

"Yes! Mr Winslow?"

"Yeah. I'm here. I'm in the city. Where are you?"

Jeff said they were hiding behind a building on Richmond Street.

"Okay, I'm on Richmond right now," John said. "I'm in my truck, the one that says 'Shady Acres' on the side."

That would be easy to spot, Jeff thought. Not just

for him, but for Harry Green. Oh well, there was only so much you could do.

"There's a big movie theatre on Richmond near where we are," Jeff said. "Why don't you wait there?"

"Got it." John ended the call.

Well?

"He's here. He's going to wait for us out the front of the movie theatre." Jeff poked his head out beyond the garbage can. "Looks safe to make our move." He got to his feet and moved out, Chipper close behind, but had barely taken a step when he stopped. "Get back, get back, get back!" he whispered to Chipper.

They threw themselves back between the tall garbage cans.

What did you see?

"Harry! He just came out of the alley!"

Can we go the other way?

"If we do, he'll see us. We have to sit tight for a while."

Jeff could feel his heart pounding in his chest. When he slipped his arm around Chipper, he could feel the dog's heart thumping quickly, too.

"If we need it, can you do your noise thing?" Jeff asked. Jeff remembered how Daggert and his team had been stunned by the ear-splitting noise Chipper could make.

Yes.

161

"Okay. If he comes this way, if he spots us, you do your thing."

Aye aye, Captain.

Jeff did a double-take when he saw Chipper's response. It was fun to see him developing a sense of humour, even in the middle of all this trouble.

Jeff peeked around the bin. Harry was walking in their direction. He stopped, put his hands around his mouth to make a tiny megaphone, and called out: "Jeff? Chipper? Are you here?"

They did not make a sound.

"If you are, you need to come out. I need to explain some things to you. I'm not a bad guy. I'm really not."

"Yeah, right," Jeff whispered in Chipper's ear.

Harry took his hands away from his mouth and resumed walking. He was getting closer with every step.

"Soon as I put my fingers in my ears," Jeff whispered, "that's the signal."

They waited.

Harry got closer.

He was no more than six steps away. With each step, he scanned from side to side. Once he reached those garbage cans, he'd definitely see them.

"Come on, Jeff! You, too, Chipper! Let me explain!"

And then Harry lowered his voice to a grumble, but he was close enough that they could hear him say to himself, "Better try the next block."

But he had not stopped and turned around. He was still coming closer.

He was one step away.

Jeff put an index finger into each of his ears. Chipper opened his mouth. And what came out was a noise so high-pitched that at least one window two floors up shattered.

They burst out of their hiding place together. Harry already had his palms pressed to the side of his head, and at the sight of Jeff and Chipper his jaw dropped.

He shouted, "Your parents are here! Your mom and dad are in the next alley! They're alive! Your mom and dad are alive!"

But not a word of what he said could be heard over what was coming out of Chipper's mouth, and besides, Jeff still had his fingers in his ears.

As they shot past Harry, Chipper caught him just under one knee, toppling him. Harry crashed into one of the garbage cans, spilling trash on to the ground.

As Jeff and the dog vanished into the city, Edwin and Patricia emerged, running, from the next alley. The ear-splitting noise had just stopped as Edwin shouted, "What happened?"

Harry shook his head, unable to hear anything but a loud ringing in his ears. But he could guess what Edwin was asking him.

Harry pointed. "That way! They went that way!"

28

Emily and Pepper had been released from their small cage and placed in a larger cage. Well, not a cage exactly. They were in a room twenty by twenty feet, and about ten feet high. Like the receiving area of The Institute, the walls were white, and the fluorescent lights hidden behind panels in the ceiling made the room seem even brighter.

"You need sunglasses in here," Emily quipped. "No wonder that Daggert dude is wearing them all the time."

There was nothing in the room. Not a chair, not a table, not even a toilet. The only thing that broke the monotony was the windowless door in one wall.

Emily noticed, in the upper corners of the room, black dots that she guessed were tiny cameras. They were being watched. That did not surprise her. Although what Daggert and that creepy Timothy, or anyone else in this building, expected to learn by watching her and this dog was a mystery to her.

Pepper had shown very little curiosity about their plight. After giving the entire room a good sniff, she had curled up in one corner, placed her head on her paws, and gone to sleep. But every time Emily moved, Pepper would open her eyes, see what she was up to, then close them again.

Pepper didn't seem the slightest bit scared, either. Emily was putting up as brave a front as she could, but in her heart, she was terrified. These Institute types were bad, bad people.

But she had to be tough. She had to be like her dad. Yes, she'd been upset with him recently, but she'd never known a man who was braver than her dad. When she was a little girl, she'd worshipped him, seeing him in his uniform, heading out every day to protect the people.

Be your dad, she thought. *Stand tall.*

It hadn't taken Emily long to figure out who her fellow captive was. She'd heard Daggert and the boy refer to her as "Pepper". She remembered Jeff telling her about the dog he'd given up after his parents died and he went to live with his Aunt Flo. That dog's name had been Pepper.

So The Institute had kidnapped her and Pepper. You didn't have to be Nancy Drew to figure out what was going on here. Emily had her doubts they would ever be released, even if Jeff brought Chipper back to them. The Institute did not strike her as the kind of organisation that kept its word.

The only one who might be spared was Pepper. She wasn't going to tell anybody anything.

Unless . . .

Emily looked at Jeff's former pet, eyes shut, sleeping peacefully. No, The Institute wouldn't let Pepper go. They'd try to turn her into another dog like Chipper. Or, more likely, Barbara. Chipper might be a product of The Institute, but he was a dog who understood right and wrong, who thought for himself. But Barbara, Emily surmised, was a dog who followed orders without question.

Emily thought about how worried her father must be. Did he have any idea what had happened to her when she didn't return to help him with the dock? Had Daggert told him not to call the police? How she wished she could get a message to him, let him know that she was – at least for now – alive.

She paced the room, wracking her brain, trying to come up with any kind of plan that would get her and Pepper out of here.

"This is bad, really bad," she said aloud, to herself. That prompted Pepper to open her eyes and watch Emily pacing the room.

Emily managed to tamp down her fear long enough to smile at her. "We haven't been properly introduced." She walked over to the dog and sat with her back to the wall, legs straight out. Pepper rested her head on Emily's knees.

The girl patted the dog's head softly. "My name is Emily, and you're Pepper."

At the mention of her name, Pepper's tail thumped.

"You don't know anything about me, but I'm a friend of Jeff's."

Now Pepper's tail started wagging.

"Yeah, you remember Jeff, don't you? He loved you so much. He felt terrible when he couldn't take you with him to his aunt's place. But then he met this other dog, named Chipper, who was a very special dog, who escaped from this very place. But just because Jeff had a new friend didn't mean he loved you any less. He still missed you."

Pepper watched Emily talk.

Emily continued to pat the dog's head. It was comforting for Emily to have Pepper there. With Pepper at her side, she was not alone, and had someone to talk to, at least until The Institute made up its mind about what it would do with them.

"You actually look a lot like Chipper. When Jeff's parents were working here, before they were killed, they were the ones to put all that special equipment into Chipper. From what I gather, they really liked Chipper, and talked to him about their son and the fishing camp, and maybe they chose Chipper for the programme because he reminded them of you. Or – I might have the order of things wrong – they picked you because you reminded them of Chipper."

She rolled her eyes. "Like any of that actually matters."

Pepper had not taken her eyes off Emily as she delivered her mini-speech. It was almost as if she understood.

"I know this doesn't make any sense to you," Emily said, "but—"

And then, all of sudden, Emily had an idea.

What if it *did* make sense to Pepper? What if Pepper did have the same abilities as Chipper?

She didn't, of course.

But The Institute didn't know that.

29

As Jeff and Chipper emerged from the alley on to the sidewalk, they looked for John Winslow's pickup truck. The movie theatre Jeff had directed him to was steps away, but there was no sign of a truck with "Shady Acres" written on the side.

Jeff glanced back into the alley. Harry Green had appeared at the far end and was waving his hands and shouting. Whatever he was yelling at them, Jeff couldn't make it out.

Anxiously, Jeff said, "Where's Mr Winslow?"

Chipper scanned the street, which was full of cars.

Jeff took another look over his shoulder. Harry Green was limping towards them. He must have hurt his leg when Chipper knocked him into that garbage can.

Jeff feared that if he and Chipper made a run for it, they'd miss their rendezvous with John. But if they continued to stand there, Harry was going to catch up with them. Jeff could ask Chipper to do his

169

noise-making stunt again to slow him down, but was it a good idea to do it out here on the sidewalk, with so many people walking by? Did they want to drop dozens of innocent passers-by to their knees?

Jeff would give Emily's dad three more seconds to show up.

One . . .

Two . . .

Jeff decided to take one last look to see how close Harry was getting. He was no more than fifty feet away, but now there were two people behind him, also running this way!

Oh no! Now Harry has help!

Jeff couldn't make them out, as Harry was blocking his view of them. But there wasn't time to look that way any longer.

"Run!" Jeff said to Chipper.

Jeff headed straight out into the street, darting in front of cars, dodging and weaving his way through vehicles. Brakes squealed, horns blared, drivers shouted. Chipper was hot on his heels. At one point, the dog even ducked under a dumper truck, running in just ahead of the right front wheel and coming out the far side behind the left one.

As horns continued to honk, and angry drivers kept shouting words that Jeff's Aunt Flo would not have approved of, one voice lifted itself above the crowd.

"Jeff!"

It was not Harry Green's voice.

Jeff stopped a few feet short of the opposite sidewalk and looked towards the voice.

It was John Winslow.

He'd stopped his truck in the middle of the street, opened the door, and was standing on the edge of the truck's frame so that his head was a good two feet above the cab.

"Jeff!" he shouted again.

"It's him!" Jeff said. He pivoted and started running back into the street. He ran around to the far side of the truck and pulled open the door. Looking to save time, Chipper ran around to the back of the truck and performed an astonishing leap from street level, over the tailgate and into the empty cargo bed.

John was getting back behind the wheel as Jeff dropped on to the seat next to him. He glanced through the rear window to make sure Chipper was aboard.

"Go!" Jeff said. "Go! Go! Go!"

Emily's dad did not wait for an explanation about why they needed to get moving immediately. There was a car stopped directly ahead of them, so he turned the wheel hard and tromped on the accelerator, doing a U-turn to steer the car into the opposite lane.

Even more cars honked as he sped off in the other direction. Jeff looked back into the cargo bed to make sure Chipper was okay. He had his legs braced far apart for balance.

"Where to?" John asked.

"Anywhere!" Jeff shouted. "Just get us out of here! Harry almost caught up with us! And he has backup!"

"Backup? What kind of backup?"

"I don't know! At least one man and a woman!"

"You ever seen them before?"

Jeff needed a moment to catch his breath. "I didn't get a good look." He took another few deep breaths. "When we get a few blocks away, stop so we can get Chipper in here."

"He's not okay back there?"

Jeff looked sternly at John. "Chipper's not some dog who rides in the back of the truck. Chipper's the brains of this operation. He knows where they've got Emily and Pepper."

John slowly shook his head. "I still can't believe we're taking our lead from a dog. Do you think Emily's okay?" John gripped the wheel so hard his knuckles looked as though they might snap. "Will they hurt her?"

Jeff didn't know what to tell him but the truth. "It's possible."

John eased the truck over to the kerb and stopped long enough for Jeff to open the door and let Chipper leap from the back of the truck to the pavement and then back into the cab.

As John hit the gas again, Jeff tumbled off the seat, his head landing on the lower cushion. That was when he noticed the gun holstered to John's belt.

"Where to?" John said for the second time, but this time he was asking Chipper.

Jeff crawled back up on to the seat and looked at his phone.

Good question.

* * *

Harry Green got to the sidewalk in time to see Jeff and Chipper leap into the pickup. Edwin and Patricia came running out of the alley so quickly they nearly knocked Harry over.

"Where is he?" Patricia asked breathlessly.

"They just got in that truck," Harry said.

The pickup was doing a U-turn in the middle of the street.

"There's something written on the door!" Edwin said.

Harry was just able to catch a glimpse of it as the truck sped away.

"Shady Acres," he said. "They're with John Winslow!"

"Who's that?" Patricia asked.

"Never mind," Harry said. "There's my van. Let's go!"

30

When Wilkins wasn't monitoring the phones of John Winslow, or Jeff Conroy's Aunt Flo, or the family that took in Pepper after the boy's parents died, and when he wasn't still trying to lock in on Chipper's location, or reviewing data from highway cameras that might spot the van that Harry Green had been driving, or even waiting for the results of the DNA test that Daggert wanted, he was checking in on The Institute's very special guests.

One of his screens was linked to the cameras mounted in the top corners of the room where Emily Winslow and Pepper were being held.

There really wasn't much to see. There was the girl, and there was the dog. But it made sense to check in on them occasionally.

Wilkins wanted to be seen to be doing a good job after making Madam Director so angry. Before she'd made him drink that scalding coffee, burning his tongue so badly he could barely speak, he'd told her how sorry he was to have said anything negative about her. He was having a bad day, he said. He was having trouble at home. His mother was sick. He thought of as many excuses as he could.

Who knew that a six year old they'd fitted with all sorts of high-tech equipment could hear through walls? Maybe it was a blessing not being able to talk, Wilkins thought. He'd get in a lot less trouble that way.

Now it was Daggert making him nervous. The security chief's request for a DNA analysis on that straw clearly had not come through Madam Director. Daggert was going behind her back in asking Wilkins for the information. What was it Daggert had said?

There's something going on, and it's just not right.

As far as Wilkins was concerned, there were a *lot* of things going on around The Institute that were just not right, but he'd never had the courage to do anything about it. That Daggert might be was rather a surprise to Wilkins.

He glanced at the screen monitoring the cell.

The girl was talking. Well, her lips were moving, so she was probably talking. She was sitting on the floor with her back to the wall, the dog curled up right next to her, looking at her.

Well, Wilkins supposed that made sense. The girl would pass the time talking to the dog.

Except . . .

The girl would say something, then pause, and tilt her head a little, as though listening to a reply. Then she'd repeat the process. Talk, pause, listen. That was definitely curious. There was no one for her to talk to. Well, okay, there was the dog to *talk* to, but there was no one to *listen* to.

Wilkins watched with puzzlement as the girl continued her obviously imaginary conversation. He slipped on his headset. The cell was equipped not just with cameras, but microphones. He brought up the volume so he could hear what Emily was saying.

". . . so they don't even have to open you up to set the thing off? Like, even if they just do an X-ray or something? That'll do it, too?"

What is she talking about? Wilkins wondered.

Now Emily had stopped talking. She appeared to be listening. She looked at Pepper and nodded two or three times.

Then she said, "How big would the explosion be?"

A pause.

"Whoa," she said. "A good part of the building?"

Another pause.

Then Emily asked, "Okay, here's what I don't get. So you were never here at The Institute, but you still got turned into a dog like Chipper?" She awaited a reply. Then, "So you're an even *more* advanced model?"

Wilkins was so engrossed by what he was hearing that he did not notice a report had just arrived in his inbox.

"So let me get this straight," Emily said. "Jeff's parents, without anyone here knowing about it, designed an even more sophisticated model – that would be *you* – that completely disguises what it is?"

Pepper looked into her eyes. Emily nodded, then said, "How can I even be hearing you in my head? With Chipper, I set up this link between his thoughts and a phone, so everything came up as a text. But with you, it's totally different. You just think it, and I hear it in my head! How is that even possible?"

Wilkins reached for his phone and entered a number. He took the headset off for a moment to put the phone to his ear.

"Hello?" said Daggert.

"It's Wilkins," he said, but his voice was barely even a whisper. He sounded like someone who, while having laryngitis, came down with a second bout of laryngitis.

"Who is this?"

"Wilkins," he breathed.

"Is this Wilkins? If it's Wilkins, tap the phone once."

Wilkins picked up a pen and tapped the mouthpiece once.

"What do you want, Wilkins?"

"Something you should see."

"What? I can't understand you. Wait, did that DNA result come in?"

Wilkins glanced at his other screen. Something had landed in the inbox while he was listening to the girl. He clicked on it.

"Yes," he whispered.

"Did you say yes?"

Wilkins tapped the mouthpiece once with his pen.

"Okay, I'll be right there. Was there something else?"

Wilkins tapped again.

"What?"

Wilkins cleared his throat, hoping that would help. "The girl," he said.

"What about – never mind, I'm on my way."

Daggert ended the call. Wilkins slipped the headset back on and opened the report. He scanned it quickly, and thought, *Whoa*.

Emily was still talking. "So, whoever you look at, you can send them a message, even if I don't have any kind of earphone or anything? That's like, the most amazing thing *ever*."

Whoa, thought Wilkins, for the second time.

Based on what he'd heard, he tried to piece together what seemed to be going on. Clearly Pepper was also a hybrid dog, except Edwin and Patricia Conroy had developed her outside The Institute, on their own, without anyone here knowing.

Why would they have done that?

Were they getting ready to surprise Madam Director with this advanced dog but they never had a chance because they died in that plane crash? Or had they been developing an even more amazing model that they could sell to someone else?

But there was something even more amazing about this, if Wilkins had heard what he thought he'd heard.

If anyone tried to tinker with Pepper, to open her up, even to X-ray her to see what was inside, she would blow up.

31

John Winslow glanced into his rear-view mirror and said, "Oh no."

"What?" said Jeff.

"I think we've got a tail."

Jeff spun around to look out the back window, which, given that it was a pickup truck, was right in front of his nose. There was a sliding pane within the window that could be opened.

"It's Harry Green's van!" Jeff said. "I can see him behind the wheel!"

"Is he alone?"

"Hard to tell," Jeff said.

Let me have a look.

Chipper got his paws up on the back of the seat and stared intently at the van, which was about five hundred feet behind them.

"Can you, like, magnify with those eyes of yours?" Jeff asked.

Yes.

"Has Harry got help?"

Yes.

"There were two people with him in the alley."

I can make out two more humans in the van. One in the seat up front, one further back. A man and a woman.

"Can you see who they are? Is the man Daggert?"

Maybe. I cannot be sure.

"We need to lose them!" Jeff told Emily's father.

"This truck isn't exactly a Ferrari," John Winslow said.

"Well, that van isn't exactly a Corvette," Jeff said. "It's an old Volkswagen camper van and, believe me, it is not built for speed."

They had been circling the city on a four-lane highway bypass, discussing how they might get into The Institute to rescue Emily and Pepper, when they'd spotted Harry tailing them.

"There's no real way to lose them here," John said. "No side streets, no tunnels, nothin'. I'd have to head back into the downtown area to lose them, and might end up getting stuck in traffic. Then we'd be sitting ducks."

Jeff and Chipper had their eyes on the van. But then Jeff glanced down at the gun holstered to John's belt.

"I have an idea," Jeff said.

"What's that?" Emily's dad said.

"We shoot out their tyres."

John glanced at Jeff and followed his eye down to his belt. "Kid, do you even know how to fire a gun?"

"No," said Jeff. "But I know how to drive."

John blinked.

Jeff said, "Mr Winslow, remember the first time you met me? It was at the dump. I was unloading all the garbage from my aunt's place."

"I remember."

"Then you'll also remember I drove up there on my own."

Emily's father glanced at him. "What are you proposing?"

"You shoot, I'll drive."

"You ever driven on a major road like this? Going this fast?" At that moment they were doing sixty miles per hour.

Jeff recalled he'd told Chipper only a short while ago there was no way he could drive in city conditions. But certain circumstances could make you change your mind.

"I can do it," Jeff said. "We just have to switch positions."

"Yeah, well, that should be a piece of cake," the man said, shaking his head. "Okay, when you were a little kid, did your dad ever let you sit on his lap while he was driving and let you pretend you were doing it?"

"Yes, sir."

"You're a not a little kid any more, but we're going to try the same thing now, because you're still a lot lighter than I am. You get yourself on my lap, get hold of the wheel, and then I'll shift myself out from under you. Now, there's going to be a few seconds when I have to take my foot off the gas, and they're going to gain on us, but once you're in position, floor it."

"Got it."

Chipper, who had been in the middle of the seat, leapt over Jeff and took a position by the passenger side window as Jeff shifted closer to Emily's dad.

"It's gonna be tight," Jeff said, as he shifted himself up on to John's lap. The steering wheel pressed hard into his thighs.

"Okay, grab the wheel. You got it?"

"I've got it!"

"Okay, on three. One . . . two . . . three!"

John shifted his body hard to the middle of the cab, allowing Jeff to drop into position. The truck suddenly slowed. Chipper, looking behind them, saw the van suddenly take a leap forward in their direction.

Jeff was not as tall as Emily's father, so his foot did not immediately reach the pedal. He had to shift his butt forward to get his foot on the gas. But once he had it there, he pressed down hard and the pickup's engine roared. The truck shot forward.

"Yeah!" Jeff cried.

John turned around in the seat so he was on his knees looking backward. He moved the pane in the rear window to the side. Fresh air whipped around the inside of the cab. He took out his gun and stuck his arm out the window, aiming it towards the passenger-side front tyre of Harry Green's van.

"Okay, kid," he shouted. "When I pull the trigger, it's gonna be loud. Just concentrate on your job. Keep a good hold on that wheel, and keep the pedal to the metal!"

"Don't worry about me!" Jeff said. "I've got this!"

Jeff realised, at that moment, a part of him was having *fun*.

* * *

Edwin Conroy, sitting in the front passenger seat next to Harry Green, said, "What's going on up there?"

Patricia, seated at the small table in the middle of the camper van, leaned forward, trying to get a better look.

"Is . . . Jeff trying to switch positions with that man?"

"Looks like it," Harry said.

"Why would they be doing that?" Edwin asked.

Harry was shaking his head. "Hang on . . . they've done it. Jeff is driving! And it looks like . . ."

"That man – Winslow, you said? – is turning around," Edwin said.

"He's opening the little window," Patricia said. "And he's – is that what I think it is?"

184

Harry said. "It's a—"

And then they heard the shot. A bullet hit the bottom right corner of the windshield and buried itself into the dashboard. The glass spider-webbed from where the bullet had gone through.

Harry twisted the wheel hard left, then hard right, then left again, swerving wildly to avoid the next shot.

"It's us!" Patricia screamed frantically, as if anyone in the truck ahead could hear her. "Jeff, it's us!"

32

When Daggert arrived, Wilkins took the recorded surveillance footage of Emily and Pepper back to the beginning.

"What's going on?" Daggert asked.

Wilkins pointed to the screen, a frozen image of the girl and the dog, and handed Daggert his headset. Once Daggert had it on, Wilkins hit PLAY.

Daggert stared at the screen as he listened to Emily's one-sided conversation with the dog. The girl certainly gave the appearance of listening to what the dog had to say.

Daggert whipped off the headset and threw it on to Wilkins' keyboard. "It must be a trick."

Wilkins shrugged an *I'm not so sure* gesture.

"What do you mean?" Daggert asked. "You mean because that dog once belonged to the Conroys?" Before Wilkins could offer another gesture, Daggert said, "I need to talk to the girl."

Then, recalling his earlier request, he lowered his voice and asked, "What about that DNA thing?"

Wilkins opened another file on his screen. It was so dense with text Daggert waved a dismissive hand and said, "No time now. I'll have a look at it later."

Daggert left the control room and headed to a lower level of the building, into a maze of hallways, finally arriving at a sliding panel in the wall. There was a button on it, which he pressed, and the door slid open.

Emily and Pepper, who'd been doing some walking to stretch their legs, retreated to the far corner of the cell. Emily slid down, her back to the wall, and Pepper rested her head on her lap.

"You," Daggert said, pointing to Emily. "I want to talk to *you*."

Emily said, "Let me check my schedule and see if I have an opening."

Daggert blinked. He did not like this kid.

"I think a spot just opened up," he said.

"Well then, you picked a good time," she said, running her hand over Pepper's head.

"Tell me about this dog," he said.

"Her name is Pepper," Emily said.

"Tell me more."

"If you don't take her outside soon for a walk there's going to be a mess in here. Actually, she might not be the only one making a mess. I thought cells were supposed to be equipped with bathroom facilities? This is all going in my TripAdvisor review, just so you know."

Daggert sighed. Why, lately, was he having to deal with so many smart-alecky kids?

"We've been watching you," he said.

"What?" She acted surprised.

Daggert pointed to the black dots in the corners of the ceiling. "We've been watching and listening."

"Creepy," Emily said, eyeing him disapprovingly. "That's very inappropriate."

"Why have you been talking to the dog?" he asked.

"There's not exactly anyone else to talk to, is there? Now you're here, but to be honest, I think I'd still rather talk to the dog."

"You weren't just talking to the dog. You appeared to be having a conversation."

Emily slowly shook her head. "Uh, what?"

"Was the dog talking to you?"

Emily laughed. "Seriously? Uh, dogs can't talk except in cartoons, genius."

"Don't play dumb. You already know about Chipper. You know what he can do. So you know it's possible for a dog—a dog that has been modified—to communicate."

"Yeah, well, not this one."

"I guess we'll just have to see about that." Daggert moved towards the dog. Pepper jumped up, turned on Daggert and growled.

When Daggert went to reach for something in his pocket, Emily sprang to her feet and screamed, "I wouldn't do that!"

Daggert paused. "And why wouldn't you?"

"Just don't shoot Pepper! Not with a real gun or one of your stun gun things! Don't even get close to her! You'll be sorry!"

Daggert grinned. "Yeah, well, we'll see about that."

As he reached into his pocket again, Emily ran for the other corner, away from Pepper, and dropped into a huddle, her face to the wall, arms over her head.

Daggert brought his hand back out of his pocket, empty. He gave the dog a long, lingering appraisal.

"Okay, kid, level with me. What's going on here?"

Emily peered over her shoulder. When she saw nothing in Daggert's hand, she slowly stood.

"She'll blow up," Emily said.

"Explain."

"The Conroys realised they'd made a mistake with Chipper. If he ever fell into, like, enemy hands, they could take him apart and see what made him tick. They'd learn all The Institute's secrets."

Pepper had stopped growling and had sidestepped closer to Emily.

"It's like, one time my dad was watching the news about one of the government's planes crashing in a country we were fighting with? And instead of letting the enemy examine the plane, the government blew it up. So no one would learn how the plane worked. It's like that with Pepper."

"You're making this up."

Emily ignored that and continued. "It makes sense, actually. I'm surprised they didn't do it with Chipper. Think about it. If you brainiacs here had installed something like that in Chipper, you wouldn't have to be running all over the place trying to get him back. I mean, that's why you're trying to get him back, right? Because you don't want anyone else to find out what makes him tick. But suppose you'd ordered the self-destruct option for him? And you could activate it from here? You press a button and boom! Problem solved."

Daggert believed The Institute had actually been considering something like that at one time. He considered whether the girl could be telling the truth.

"Okay," he said slowly. "Let's say I wanted to believe you. A lot of what you're saying doesn't add up. First, how is the dog communicating with you?'

Emily shrugged, like she didn't care that she didn't know the answer. "I guess whoever Pepper wants to talk to gets to hear her. I think she has this way of projecting her thoughts. We made a kind of mental connection when you put us together in that cage."

Daggert shook his head. "I'm not buyin' it. If she can blow herself up, why hasn't she already done it?"

"Duh," Emily said. "Because she likes me. And she didn't want to blow up a little kid. That partner of yours, Timothy? But now that we're here, there's no telling what Pepper will do. In fact, you take one step closer to her, you try to grab her and find out what's inside, and I think she's gonna blow. I've told her to do what she has to do. Don't worry about me."

Daggert did not know how to call it.

Emily, seeing that she had the man's attention, added, "Now let's talk about you letting us walk out of here."

33

"Nuts!" John Winslow shouted. "I hit the windshield! I don't want to kill them! I just want them to back off!"

Jeff had his chest up against the steering wheel so that his foot could stay on the gas pedal. They were doing more than seventy miles per hour. Jeff had never driven this fast in his life, not even close. He never got Aunt Flo's pickup above forty on the way to the dump.

But his first high-speed driving experience looked as though it was about to come to an end.

Up ahead, traffic had come to a complete stop. Beyond the stopped cars, Jeff could see a dumper truck backing across the road. There had to be some construction going on up there.

Jeff didn't see how he could stop. If he stopped, the van would catch up with them.

"Uh, Mr Winslow?" he said, thinking maybe this would be a good time to seek some advice.

But Emily's dad did not respond. He had his head half out the back window, trying to line up another shot. He was aiming lower, clearly hoping to hit a tyre on their pursuers' vehicle this time, not the windshield.

Jeff realised he was going to have to solve this problem on his own.

There was a broad, grassy central reservation between the road Jeff was on and the lanes going in the other direction.

"Hang on!" Jeff said, and without letting up on the gas, he steered the pickup off the road, over the left shoulder, and onto the grass.

The truck shook and rattled. Mr Winslow pulled his head back into the cab and Chipper fell into the footwell in front of the passenger seat. Jeff could barely hold on to the steering wheel as he drove the truck over the rough ground.

But the plan was working. He was zooming past all the stopped cars.

John quickly took in the scene. The stopped cars, the looming construction, and the wide-open road beyond. And behind them, also veering off the road and on to the central reservation, was the van.

"Keep going, Jeff!" John shouted.

If Jeff could have seen his phone, currently stuck underneath him, he would have seen another encouraging message.

You are the man!

Jeff gripped the wheel so tightly he thought his fingers would break. They were past the cars now, and the dumper truck. Jeff steered the truck back towards the road. The vehicle lurched and the tyres squealed as it landed on a firmer footing.

Jeff glanced in the mirror and saw that the van was doing its best to keep up.

Once both vehicles were back on the main road, John positioned himself at the rear window again, ready to try again to shoot out the tyres.

But now Harry Green's van was weaving all over the road, making it a very difficult target.

"They're making it harder now!" John said, propped backwards on the truck's seat, his right arm – the one holding the gun – extended through the open back window.

He aimed, but every time he thought he had a tyre in his sights, the van swerved. "Can you go any faster?" John asked Jeff.

"Are you kidding?" The truck was already rattling to the point it sounded like it would fly apart.

Chipper, who'd bounded up from the footwell and now had his eyes trained on the van, was still trying to get a good look at the two other people with Harry.

The man in the passenger seat next to Harry appeared to be putting down his window.

"Uh oh," said John. "Harry's friend may have some firepower of his own. He's getting ready to lean out of the window." The man, having lowered his window, stuck his head out. The strong wind blew his hair back. It even had the effect of blowing back his lips and baring his teeth.

The man was shouting something. They couldn't hear him, but it looked like: "Stop!"

Chipper focused on the man. There was something about him.

It couldn't be.

Emily's dad fired.

Harry Green's van lurched hard towards the gravel shoulder. The man who'd been sticking his head out of the window pulled it back in.

"Ha!" John shouted. "I hit the tyre! I don't believe it! Take *that*!"

Harry struggled to maintain control. Even with one tyre shot out, he was still pushing the van to keep up with them. Shreds of rubber flew off the tyre on the passenger side.

Chipper began barking. He sent a message to Jeff.

Stop!

Then he sent another message.

Let them catch us!

Chipper glanced over at Jeff to see why he was not responding. The boy had his eyes on the road and was unaware that he was sitting on his phone. Chipper saw the edge of it sticking out from under him, and stuck his snout down there to retrieve it.

195

"Hey!" Jeff said, glancing down at the dog for a millisecond. "You mind?"

But then he saw Chipper trying to get at the phone. He'd pulled it out far enough for Jeff to see the most recent message.

Forgive me for being rude.

John was still focused on shooting out another tyre. "If I can get one I can get two!"

Jeff tightened his grip on the wheel with his left hand and reached down for the phone with his right.

Pull over!

"Why?" Jeff shouted.

"Why what?" John said.

"I'm talking to Chipper!"

Trust me! Pull over!

Jeff looked from the phone and into Chipper's eyes. He glanced at the road ahead for half a second to make sure he wasn't about to run into anything, and then once again at Chipper.

The dog slowly nodded his head.

"For real," Jeff said.

Chipper nodded again.

Jeff eased his foot off the gas.

"What are you doing?" John Winslow asked. "Don't tell me we're out of gas!"

"No," Jeff said. "Chipper says we need to pull over."

"He what?"

Jeff looked at Chipper one last time and asked, "You're sure?"

Words came up on the phone.

Positive.

Jeff said to John. "I trust him. I'm stopping."

John Winslow didn't know what to say.

Once the truck was down to thirty miles an hour, Jeff steered it over on to the gravel shoulder, kicking up a cloud of dust. He brought it to a stop, and saw in his mirror that Harry had pulled over, too, about five car lengths behind them.

"Let's take this real careful," John said.

John got out first, followed by Chipper. Jeff climbed down from the driver's side, phone in hand. The three of them gathered around the truck's tailgate and watched as Harry got out of the Volkswagen. He lifted his hands into the air in a gesture of surrender.

"Jeff!" he yelled. "It's okay!"

The passenger door opened and the man who'd been sticking his head out of the window stepped out. Seconds later, a woman followed.

Jeff blinked.

I am not seeing this, he thought.

"It's a trick!" he said suddenly. "It's some kind of trick. It can't be them! Back in the truck!"

Jeff turned, heading for the pickup's cab, but Chipper had set off in the other direction. When he was within five feet of the man and the woman, he stopped and raised his head and sniffed the air. He took a few tentative steps closer, then put his nose down to the man's shoes. Then he moved over to the woman and sniffed her feet.

Jeff, his hand on the driver's door, his heart beating so hard he could hear it, looked at his phone.

They smell right!

"Who are they?" John asked, as Chipper wagged his tail so hard his entire body was gyrating. The dog was leaping at the two with such excitement that he was interfering with their attempts to run to Jeff.

Jeff said woozily, "That's my mom and dad."

And then he passed out and collapsed to the ground.

34

"That is, indeed, an interesting development," Madam Director said.

Daggert stood in front of her, her desk separating them. He had brought up her up to speed on his conversation with Emily Winslow.

"Is it possible?" Daggert asked. "Could Edwin and Patricia Conroy have been working on something without telling us? A dog with that capability?"

"It is *possible*," she said, shaking her head. "I don't think they could have done that work here, without our knowing it. They must have set up a lab in their house. How devious of them if it's true. If we hadn't already killed them, I'd want it done immediately. What do you suppose their plan was?"

"Maybe – just maybe, they were going to surprise you with their new development," Daggert said, "but I think it's more likely they were going to sell it to the highest bidder."

"Of course, the other possibility," Madam Director said, "is that the girl is bluffing."

"Agreed. But in the meantime, I've cleared that end of The Institute of personnel. If the dog does detonate, damage will be minimal, except in the cell itself."

"There is a way to get close to the dog and assess its capabilities without setting it off," she said.

"Yes?"

"Timothy," she said.

"Timothy?"

She nodded. "His hearing is so acute, Timothy should be able to hear the components operating within the animal. Just as within any laptop, there are cooling mechanisms that create an almost imperceptible whirring sound. Put Timothy in the room and let him listen. If he hears nothing, we know the girl is an inventive liar."

Daggert nodded. "And what if the girl is not an inventive liar, and the dog detects Timothy trying to listen in on his operating system?"

Madam Director pursed her lips momentarily, then made two fists and held them in the air. She opened her fingers suddenly and said, "*Kaboom*. No more Timothy. But we're already gearing up to make more just like him."

Daggert had not always enjoyed his time with his tiny partner, but he wasn't sure he wished him that fate.

Madam Director was not finished. "The only reason we have the girl and the other dog here is to lure back H-1094 and the Conroy boy. Once that's done, it doesn't matter what happens to any of them."

Daggert stood there a moment before finally saying, "I'll keep you posted."

* * *

Back in the control room, Daggert found Wilkins again.

"Watson," he said, rolling a chair over and sitting down next to him.

Even if Wilkins had his voice, he was too tired to correct Daggert.

"You said you had something back from that straw I had you test?"

Wilkins struggled to speak. "I did the test. I got two hits."

"Two hits?"

Wilkins nodded. He called up the report on to his screen. Daggert found himself looking at things he did not understand. Helixes, bar graphs, charts.

"What's this?"

Wilkins waved away the question. "You wouldn't understand," he whispered

"What did you say? No, don't try to talk louder," Daggert said, glancing over this shoulder. "You never know where Timothy will be."

201

Wilkins pointed to the screen and whispered. "You gave me a straw he used. I found his DNA."

Daggert nodded. "Right. I didn't want to tell you. I wanted to see if you came up with that on your own. I guess it's somewhat reassuring to find out he's a real boy, and not some advanced form of artificial intelligence. Now, what else you got?"

Wilkins pointed and said, "This."

"What?"

"*This.*"

"Have you thought of sucking on some cough drops? That might help."

Wilkins kept pointing to the screen and a line of text reading: "*50% match.*"

"So what does that mean? You found someone with fifty per cent of matching DNA?"

Wilkins nodded.

"So what would that be? A parent? His mother or father?"

Wilkins nodded again.

"So one of his parents is actually in our database?" Daggert asked. The Institute was able to link in with databases all over the world. If there was someone out there – anywhere – whose DNA profile was in a computer, The Institute would be able to find them.

Wilkins nodded yes to Daggert's last question. He pointed to the screen one more time.

There were details about the DNA match.

Age: 37

Sex: Male

Employer: The Institute.

"Wait, what?" Daggert said. "It's someone here? In this building?

Wilkins pointed to the last line. Daggert leaned in, then blinked several times, not sure he was seeing things properly.

"Daggert?" he said, reading his own name. "The match is with . . . me?"

Wilkins struggled to be able to say just three words. "He's your son."

Daggert stared at the screen, disbelieving.

Was it possible? Could Timothy really be . . .

And then he thought of a woman named Diane, from seven years earlier. The woman he'd left behind. She never said a thing. If she had told him . . .

I'm a father?

Timothy is my son?

Daggert was overcome by the news. First of all, he was just plain shocked, almost to the point of being dizzy. But he also felt . . . pride? Yes, that was it. He was *proud* that he was a father. His chest seemed to swell under his suit jacket.

But then he felt something else.

Anger started to build within him.

How dare they do that to my boy? How dare they turn him into a . . . thing?

But it was even worse than that.

To test Pepper's capabilities, Madam Director was willing to risk having Timothy blown to bits.

35

"Jeff! Wake up!"

"Jeff! It's me! It's Mom!"

"Come on, come on, wake up, son!"

Edwin and Patricia had gone down on their knees on either side of Jeff as he lay beside the truck next to the highway.

"Jeff!" Patricia said. "It's really us! It's not a trick!"

Edwin lifted the boy up enough that he could cradle him in his arms. He put his mouth to Jeff's ear and whispered, "We thought about you every minute of every day. It's me, Jeff. It's your dad."

But Jeff was still out cold. The shock of seeing his parents alive had caused him to faint, and he'd bumped the back of his head when he hit the ground. Patricia felt around in his hair for blood but found none.

Chipper had an idea.

He stepped up to Jeff and gave him a big slobbery lick from chin to forehead. Even before regaining full consciousness, Jeff made a face like he'd just been forced to eat a plateful of broccoli.

"Blecch!" he said, then opened his eyes. Once they'd focused on his parents, they went even wider.

Patricia's grin stretched from ear to ear. "If I'd known that would work I'd have licked you."

Jeff looked disbelievingly at her, then at his father, then back again to his mother.

"How can you . . . what . . . where have you . . ."

Jeff was incapable of forming one simple question, and seemed to be bordering on delirious. He forced himself to concentrate, and managed one coherent question.

"Is this a dream?" he asked.

Edwin and Patricia, tears running down their faces, shook their heads and said in unison, "No."

Jeff lunged forward and threw his arms wide enough to grab them both around the neck. All three were crying and squeezing each other, and even John Winslow and Harry Green, standing a few feet away, could not stop themselves from getting choked up.

Chipper took a respectful step back and let the Conroy family enjoy their long-overdue reunion.

When, after several seconds, they untangled themselves from each other, Jeff asked, "How? The plane crash? What happened? Did you have parachutes?"

Jeff's parents got him to his feet, checked him all over to make sure he was okay, then led him around the truck and on to the grass. The ground sloped up, and the three of them found a comfortable perch on the side of the hill.

Edwin and Patricia, taking turns, explained to Jeff what had happened. How they decided not to get on the plane, and when it exploded, realised they were supposed to have died. They believed if The Institute knew they were alive, they would hunt them down, and Jeff would never be safe. So, painful as it was, they pretended to be dead, hoping one day there'd be a way to resume their old lives, to neutralise the threat against them, and be reunited with Jeff. They got their friend Harry Green to keep an eye on him.

Good thing, too.

"I think," Patricia said to her son, "that we spoke of you so much when we were working with Chipper, and with such love, that when he escaped, he felt a need to find and protect you. He would have thought, as everyone else did, that we were dead."

Jeff had his phone back in his hand and noticed some text pop up.

That is true. I cared about you even before I found you.

Jeff looked ready to tear up again. Chipper was wagging his tail and almost seemed to be smiling.

"Why?" Jeff asked his parents.

"Why what?" Patricia said.

"Why did The Institute want to kill you? Chipper told me you'd found out about something they were going to do, but he didn't know what."

Edwin and Patricia exchanged looks, as if checking with each other about whether it was safe to tell their son what their former bosses were up to. They shrugged almost at the same time, as if to say, *At this point, what does it matter?*

Patricia said, "They wanted to do to children what they had done to Chipper."

Jeff's eyes went wide, but before he could respond, John Winslow cut in.

"Look, I hate to interrupt, but we're not getting Emily back standing here."

"Emily?" said Patricia.

"My daughter," John said through gritted teeth. "They've got my girl. And I'm going to get her back, with or without your help."

Edwin paled. "This is horrible. Harry told us The Institute had Pepper, but they took your girl?"

John nodded grimly.

"That was our next move," Jeff said. "Figuring out how to get them both back. Chipper was working on a plan."

Patricia looked to the dog. Jeff held up his phone so she could see his response.

Some of the details are yet to be worked out.

"You're supposed to be a pretty smart dog," she said, "but if *you* don't even have a plan . . ."

"What are you saying?" John asked angrily. "It can't be done? We can't get my daughter back?"

Edwin said, "They obviously want to make a trade. Chipper, for Emily and Pepper. How were you supposed to get back to them, anyway?"

Jeff smiled cautiously and raised a finger into the air . . .

"Now that the team is all back together," he said, "I think I might have an idea."

* * *

Not long after that, Jeff and Chipper were on the road again, with Harry at the wheel.

In a van that was about to become airborne.

36

Daggert left The Institute and walked out into the gardens that helped hide the building from the city that surrounded it. He got out his cell phone and entered a number he'd not called in years.

"Hello?" a woman said after the fourth ring.

"Diane?" Daggert said.

There was a pause at the other end of the line, as though the woman was holding her breath.

"Bobby?" she said hesitantly. Daggert could think of no one else who called him by his first name. Hardly anyone knew what it was.

"Yes," he said.

"It's been seven years," she said. "You vanished from my life."

"I . . . I'm sorry about that," Daggert said. "My work. I had to go."

"Your work was always so mysterious."

"I never told you how sorry I was," he said.

"Your apology is a little late," she said. "I'm married now, Bobby. I've moved on."

"Good, good. Listen, there's something I have to ask you."

"What?"

"After I left . . . were you, I mean, were you . . ."

There was silence at the other end of the line. Then, the sound of someone crying.

"Diane?"

Some sniffling, and then, "Yes."

Daggert asked, "What happened?"

"I . . . I gave him up. For adoption."

"Do you know where he was placed?"

"No," she said. "I thought it was better not to know. Why are you asking me—"

Daggert ended the call. He'd found out what he needed to know.

* * *

Timothy found Daggert in his private office, sitting behind his desk.

"I've been looking for you," Timothy said.

Daggert stared at the boy without saying anything.

"What's wrong?" Timothy asked.

"Nothing," Daggert said.

"You're looking at me funny," the boy said. "Have I got a wire sticking out of my head or something?"

"No, nothing like that. In fact, you look just fine. You're a fine-looking young man." Daggert smiled sadly.

Timothy blinked a couple of times. "Okay. Good to know, I guess. So what were you doing?"

"Nothing much. Just making a phone call." Daggert paused. "Let me ask you something, Timothy."

The boy shrugged. "Sure."

"If you could find out who your real parents were, or maybe even just one of them, would you want to know?"

Timothy thought about that. "I don't know. It's not like I'd ever get to see them or anything, now that I'm working for The Institute. What would be the point?"

"Well, let's say—"

"Anyway," Timothy said, cutting him off, "Madam Director sent me to get you. Jeff's been in touch."

"What?"

"He's made contact. Through the dog. He wants to know how to go about the switch. The girl and the other dog for H-1094. But he says he won't bring H-1094 to us until we've released them." Timothy smiled. "I don't think that's part of Madam Director's plan."

"No," Daggert said quietly. "I don't imagine it is."

"When Jeff made contact, we got a lock on his position. We know where they are, but they're on the move. I'm staying here, but there's a chopper warming up for you. Madam Director said something about it being The Institute's new pick-up service."

37

The van was lifting off the road. Thick black straps, like immense strands of dark pasta, had been dangling from the overhead helicopter. Jeff was reminded of the thick brushes in a car wash, but these straps were not made of rubber or fabric. They were clearly magnetic, because once they got close to the van, they were drawn to it. Each strap attached to the vehicle with a resounding slap. Five on one side, five on the other.

"I've never seen anything like this!" Harry shouted from behind the wheel.

Harry tried yanking the wheel back and forth, not unlike how he'd been doing when John Winslow had been shooting at them. But it didn't make any difference. The tyres were no longer in contact with the road.

"What the—" said Harry.

Chipper, his head sticking out the window, watched as the road beneath them drifted away. Soon they were able to see the tops of trees and the roofs of houses. Then he looked up, and was pretty sure he could make out, in the front bubble of the helicopter, Daggert.

But Daggert was not piloting. A man sat next to him at the controls. Daggert had an index finger pointed up. He spun it in a circle, then pointed it in the direction from which they'd come.

The helicopter banked. As it started heading back, the van swung out in a wide arc, forcing Jeff and Harry to hang on tightly. Jeff pulled Chipper back from the window so he would not fall out.

"Where are they taking us?" Jeff shouted over the roar of the helicopter's blades.

"The Institute, I guess!" Harry shouted. "Where else? Unless they decide to take us out over the ocean and drop us in!"

Jeff hadn't thought of that. "Which way is the ocean?"

Harry shook his head. "I've kind of lost my bearings, kid!"

As the helicopter settled into its new route, things got back to normal inside the van. The view was spectacular, but no one was in a mood to enjoy it. They were about half a mile up. The sky was clear, and they could see for miles.

Within minutes, they were over the city.

"Chipper," Jeff said, "do you know where we are? Is this the way to The Institute?"

Yes.

Jeff nodded knowingly. "When you dropped your message-blocking system so we could tell them we were ready to talk, you purposely left it down long enough to let them lock in on us." He paused. "Just like I figured."

Looking ahead through the front windshield, a building that was both industrial and elegant came into view. It sat on a large tract of land that occupied several city blocks but still contained large wooded areas and much greenery. Even at their altitude, a high perimeter fence and large iron gate could be seen.

"Is that it?" Jeff asked.

Chipper nodded.

"Are you scared about going back in there?"

Chipper hesitated before replying.

I hope I am not so frightened that I pee a little.

Jeff put his arm around the dog and pulled him close. "You and me both, pal."

They were now flying over The Institute grounds. Slowly, they began to descend. The helicopter dropped several hundred feet, then hovered over what was clearly the back of the building, judging by the presence of loading docks and Dumpsters.

The chopper gently lowered the van to the ground. Once the tyres touched pavement, the magnetic bands that had attached themselves to the vehicle went slack and retracted. They rose into the air and disappeared into a box on the underside of the helicopter.

"Should we make a run for it?" Jeff asked.

Harry pointed to half a dozen men and women in black clothes standing only a few feet away.

"Not much point," he said.

Chipper barked and walked in frantic, tight circles inside the van.

"Stay calm, boy," Jeff said.

The helicopter settled on to a pad about a hundred feet away. As the rotors slowed, the door opened and Daggert got out. He started walking, slowly and deliberately, towards the van.

"I guess this is it," Harry said.

Daggert reached the van. He stood by the driver's door and said to Harry, "Get out."

Resignedly, Harry did as he was told. He looked like a man who'd given up the fight. Daggert moved to the side door, glared at Jeff and Chipper, and said, "Now you two."

Jeff stepped out and waited for Chipper to jump out and sit next to him before closing the door behind him.

"It's been a while," Daggert said to Jeff.

"Yeah," Jeff said. "Haven't seen you since your boat blew up."

Daggert grimaced, but said nothing.

"Hey, we've got a deal, right?" Harry Green said.

"We give you Chipper here, and you let the girl and Jeff's old dog and us go."

Daggert smiled. "Why don't we go inside and discuss it?"

Ushered by Daggert and the others, Jeff, Harry and Chipper were taken into the building through one of the back doors.

The van was left unattended.

A few minutes later, the mattress on the tiny bed at the back of the van began to rise, and a hand appeared.

Edwin Conroy crawled out from the storage area below the bed, careful to stay under the windows. Patricia, who had been crammed in next to him, followed.

"I feel like a sardine," she whispered.

Edwin slowly opened the cabinet below the tiny counter where the camper van's sink was located. John Winslow was folded in on himself, knees to chest, his head bent down under the sink.

"This must be how an elephant in a bathtub feels," John said. As he worked to get himself out of the hiding spot, he asked, "Are we there?"

"We're there," Edwin said.

"Shh!" Patricia said.

They held their breath for nearly fifteen seconds to see if anyone was going to come and check out the noises inside the van.

"They might have been listening earlier," Edwin said quietly, "but not now."

"We'll wait a few more minutes to be sure they're well into the building," Patricia said, looking at her watch. "Then, we'll see if these still work."

She held up two security cards with black stripes on them.

"What are those?" John asked.

"Our company ID cards that open any door in The Institute," Edwin said. "I'd totally forgotten we had these until Jeff asked about them."

Patricia said, "Jeff may be right about them never being cancelled. Why cancel cards for two people who are supposedly dead?"

38

"Well, well," said Madam Director with a smile that showed off her gleaming white teeth. "Look at us, all together."

She stood with her arms crossed, the tallest person in the room in her towering heels. Daggert stood to the right of her, Timothy and Barbara on her left. Others from The Institute's security team were assembled there, as well as Wilkins, who was wearing his long, white lab coat.

Facing Madam Director were Jeff, Harry and Chipper. A strip of duct tape had been wound around the dog's snout so he couldn't make his high-pitched, disabling noise.

Madam Director looked at Harry and said, "You're a bit of a puzzle to us, but we'll figure out who you are soon enough. Unless you'd like to simply tell me."

"Just a friend," Harry said.

She smiled again. "Of course you are. Nothing more than that. A simple friend with the skills necessary to evade us all this time."

She turned her attention to Jeff, who was holding the phone he used to communicate with Chipper. "And the young Mr Conroy. We finally meet. You won't be needing this any more." She took the phone from him and tossed it into a nearby garbage can. She pouted in mock sadness. "So sorry to hear about your mommy and daddy. What a terrible tragedy, that plane crash."

Jeff's face went red with anger. Here he was, face to face with the woman who had issued the order to kill his parents. "You're a horrible, evil person," he said.

Madam Director's eyebrows shot up. "You know what I do with people who say means things about me?" Another smile. "I treat them to a nice, hot cup of coffee." She glanced at Wilkins. "Isn't that right, Wilkins?"

Wilkins said nothing.

"I don't care," Jeff said. "My mom and dad figured out what a bad person you were, and you had them killed for doing the right thing."

"You seem to know a lot about it," she said, and then turned her attention to Chipper. "I suppose H-1094 here has filled you in."

She turned and looked at the Labrador retriever standing next to Timothy. "Barbara, have you properly welcomed our new guest?"

Barbara walked forward until she was nose to nose

with Chipper, then gave him a long, slurpy lick that ran right over his nostrils.

Chipper shook his head with disgust and backed away from the other dog.

Timothy said, "Shouldn't be long now."

"What shouldn't be long?" Jeff asked. "What's he talking about?"

"Do we even have a name for that?" Madam Director asked the little boy.

"I call it Sleepy Slobber," Timothy replied.

"What?" asked Jeff, but then it all became clear.

Chipper became unsteady on his feet, swayed back and forth briefly, and dropped to the floor.

"Chipper!" Jeff cried, dropping to his knees and cradling the dog's head in his arms. "Is he dead?"

"Not yet," Madam Director said. "He's just having a little snooze. Wilkins?"

Wilkins approached and edged Jeff out of the way so he could crouch down and pick up Chipper.

"What's going on?" Jeff demanded. "What are you doing with him?"

"Getting out all that we put into him," Madam Director said.

"What does *that* mean?"

"All the hardware and software that we installed is coming out. We need to figure out where we went wrong with this one. Think of it as quality control."

"Yeah, but, how will you *do* that?" Jeff asked, tears welling up in his eyes because he was sure he knew the answer.

"Cut him open, of course," Madam Director said.

"But, can't you just plug something into him?" Jeff asked. "That little port in his collar? Find the problem that way?"

"Where's the fun in that?" she said. She snapped her fingers. "Take him away, Wilkins."

Wilkins headed for the door with a limp Chipper in his arms.

"No!" Jeff cried. He made a move to take off after Wilkins, but Harry Green grabbed his arm.

"Jeff," he said, his voice calm. "There's nothing we can do." His voice lowered to a whisper. "Right now."

"*Chipper!*" Jeff cried, ignoring Harry, as the door closed and Chipper disappeared from view.

"Oh, please," Madam Director said. "If there's one thing there's too much of in this world, it's sentiment. Wouldn't you agree, Daggert?"

Daggert, stone-faced, looked at her, and then at Timothy, and said, "Whatever you say, Madam Director."

She detected something in his tone, and asked, "Are we okay today, Daggert?"

"I'm fine."

"A little airsick from the helicopter ride?"

"I said I'm fine. Although I'd like to have a word with you about something."

Madam Director's eyebrows rose again. "Oh. Well, not in front of the children. Let's park our guests first and then we can chat. Take these two and put them with the others."

Daggert nodded, then stepped forward and said to Jeff and Harry, "This way."

As they made their way down a long hallway, Jeff thought he could hear sounds of laughter and playing. The sounds grew louder the further down the hall they progressed.

When they passed a door with a large glass window Jeff stopped and peered in. What he saw made him draw a breath.

The room was decorated just like a nursery school or kindergarten classroom. Small tables, tiny chairs, blue plastic tubs filled with toys, a blackboard with the alphabet written on it.

The place was full of children.

A dozen of them. Six boys and six girls. Three were engaged in finger-painting, two were driving toy trucks in a raised sandbox on legs, four were kicking a football amongst themselves, two were stretched out on woven floor mats, on the verge of sleep as they stared at the ceiling, and the last one was off in a corner, absorbed in a picture book.

There was also a man standing in the corner. At

first Jeff figured he had to be the teacher, but then he reconsidered. This man, in a black suit, white shirt and tie, looked more like security. He wasn't doing any teaching. He was guarding.

"Move along," Daggert said.

But Jeff's curiosity held him in place. "Are those kids you've turned into robots?"

Daggert said. "Not yet." He paused. "So far, there's just the one."

"That kid I just saw you with?" Jeff asked.

"Timothy," Daggert said slowly. "Yes."

Jeff shook his head. "This is a really sick place."

Daggert said nothing, and merely pointed ahead, indicating it was time to move on. Before long, they reached a set of stairs and descended to a lower level where they were told to stop by a door with a sign on it reading "Holding Cell".

Daggert pressed a button beside the door, prompting it to retract into the wall. "In here," he said, gesturing.

Jeff and Harry walked into the room and immediately spotted Emily and Pepper sitting in the corner.

Jeff cried out, "Emily! Pepper!"

He barely noticed the door shutting behind him as Pepper sprinted across the room and jumped on him. She licked his face furiously and her body shook from her frantic tail-wagging.

"You remember me!" he said. "I didn't forget you, either!" As he embraced Pepper he looked beyond her

224

to Emily. "Hey," he said, reaching out a hand, his face turning sad again.

She gave his hand a squeeze. "Hey," she said.

"Sorry about all this," he said.

"Where's Chipper?" she asked.

Jeff's head dropped. Harry stepped forward and said, "They took him away. They're going to open him up, take out all his gadgetry."

Emily put a hand over her mouth. Her eyes went wide. "Oh no," she said.

"He always said he wanted to be rid of all that stuff," Jeff said, as Pepper calmed down. "But he wanted to be rid of it, and still be *alive*."

"I don't know what to say," Emily said.

Jeff waved her closer and in a low voice asked, "Can we talk in here?"

She lowered her voice as well. "They listen, and there's a camera up in that corner. But if you *really* whisper, you should be okay. And let me stand in front of you so they can't see our lips move."

He brought her in close. "There are things I have to tell you."

"Likewise," she said.

"You go first."

"I've got them believing that Pepper is another dog like Chipper."

"What?"

"Yeah, but I've convinced them that her advancements

are harder to detect. And that if they try to check her out by, like, listening closely to her, or X-raying her or anything like that, she's got a self-destruct mechanism that she could activate. She could blow up half the building."

"You have *got* to be kidding me. I love Pepper, but she is, I mean, she's the dumbest dog ever."

"Yeah, well, I've at least got them worried. I told them your parents rigged her up that way on their own, without The Institute's knowledge. I figured it would buy me some time, in case they were going to just kill me and Pepper. So, what's *your* news?"

"Okay, well, first of all, and don't make a face or anything, but your dad is here."

"What?"

"I said don't make a face!" he whispered.

"They've captured him, too?"

"No! He's here with – okay, this is the other part where you have to keep a straight face – my mom and dad."

"Your – *what*?"

"They're alive. They never got on that plane. They've been hiding out. And by now they should have snuck into the building."

Emily was on the verge of tears. "My dad must have been going crazy."

"Pretty much. Chipper and I called him to help us." Jeff offered a weak smile. "He's pretty cool."

Emily felt a lump in her throat. "Yeah, he is." She sniffed, then wiped her nose with the back of her hand. "So, what now?"

"I'm not sure," Jeff said. "I've got no idea how this ends."

39

Madam Director met Daggert in the hall outside the cell where he had deposited Jeff and Harry.

"What is it you want to discuss?" she asked.

"I want you to rethink using Timothy to determine whether that other dog actually poses a threat."

"Why?"

"Well, first of all, it seems a terrible waste of resources to use an asset like Timothy as a bomb detector."

"Perhaps I have my reasons," she said.

"I'd like to hear what they are."

Madam Director's eyes narrowed. "I'm not accustomed to having my decisions challenged, Daggert."

"A decision like this involves my role as head of security."

"I see." She paused. "Timothy is one of our first experiments with underdeveloped humans."

"You mean, with children," Daggert said.

Madam Director rolled her eyes. "Whatever. The

truth is, Daggert, I'm concerned about Timothy. I think we might be having the same problem with him as we did with H-1094."

"What are you talking about?"

"I've been observing him. Watching how he interacts with others, especially you. I think he may be forming some sort of bond."

"You do?"

"The signs are subtle, but they're there. Barbara has been keeping me informed."

"Excuse me? That dog has been reporting to you?"

Madam Director nodded. "Of course. That's what these dogs *do*. And she's noticed the two of you getting along very well."

"Isn't that what's *supposed* to happen?"

She shook her head. "We can't afford to have Timothy becoming emotionally involved. And so what if he does end up getting blown up by that other dog? There may be massive tissue damage, but we can find another host for the hardware and software."

"Wait a sec," Daggert said. "Timothy is still a living, breathing child."

Madam Director rested her back against the wall and folded her arms. "Is there something I need to know about you and your new partner?" she asked.

"Is there something *you* would like to tell me?" he asked.

She moved away from the wall and put her face close to his. "All you need to know is that you work for me. That means you do what I tell you. I'll be bringing Timothy down shortly, and sending him in there. That room, in case you didn't know, is designed to contain a significant explosion. If that dog is rigged the way the girl says it is, so be it. We build another Timothy, and our other problem – of what to do with the boy and the girl and the old man – will be solved."

And with that, she turned on her significant heels and walked away.

40

Wilkins set an unconscious Chipper down on the operating table.

This was the room where the other dogs were held in cages stacked against the far wall. It had been from this room that Chipper had escaped weeks earlier when Simmons – that idiot – let the dog get the better of him. It was also in this room where procedures on the dogs were most often performed: hardware installed or – in this case – removed.

It was possible, Wilkins realised, for an animal to survive the removal of its special components, if the person performing the procedure was very careful. After all, the dog had survived the installation. But Madam Director did not seem to be terribly concerned that Chipper should survive.

The caged dogs barked furiously. They had seen this kind of thing before, and they did not like it.

There were ten dogs, and Wilkins knew work had begun on half of them. The other five, the ones doing the most barking, were still awaiting their transformation.

Wilkins peeled the duct tape off Chipper's snout. There was no risk now that Chipper would bite him or emit one of his disabling sounds. A lick from Barbara was good for at least an hour. Wilkins didn't need that much time.

Wilkins slid open a drawer beneath the table, where he found an array of stainless steel surgical knives. The scalpels sparkled under the fluorescent lights in the ceiling. He picked one up and examined it, the edge of the blade gleaming.

"This should do the trick," he said to himself.

He put on a pair of latex gloves and a surgical gown. This was, he knew, going to be messy.

This was not Wilkins' favourite part of his job. He preferred his control room duties, but he was not needed there now that the boy and the dog had been found. And Simmons had not been replaced after Madam Director had made him eat a fatal doggie treat.

Wilkins examined the point where he would make his first incision. Madam Director would want him to recover those artificial eyes. They were worth a fortune. It made sense to go in just behind Chipper's neck, where the central control unit was located.

"Sorry about this," he whispered.

The dogs' incessant barking made concentrating difficult. He turned around to tell them to shut up, but with that burnt tongue, they didn't hear him.

He would have to cope with the noise. He took a deep breath and touched the blade to the top of Chipper's head, just behind the ears. He would make a cut about three inches long, down to the collar that was virtually welded to his body.

Chipper stirred.

Wilkins froze. Was the dog coming awake? He could not do this if the dog was not completely sedated. Maybe it made more sense to increase the level of sedation before doing what he had to do.

But the dog made no further movement. Maybe it was just the animal's nerves, an involuntary reaction, Wilkins thought.

So he huddled over Chipper once again, parted his fur, touched the tip of the knife to the animal's skin, and was about to apply pressure when the fluorescent lights flickered. Wilkins glanced up. The bulbs hummed and crackled.

He needed strong, consistent lighting to perform this task. He spotted a desk lamp on a nearby table that he could move over. Wilkins put down the scalpel and went to get the lamp and move it to a closer plug socket.

In another minute, he'd have all the light he needed.

41

Once inside The Institute, Edwin, Patricia and John slipped through the first unlocked door they could find, to discuss their plan. It turned out to be a laundry room, and it was their good fortune no one was there. It was early evening, and the cleaning staff had gone home for the day.

The good news was, Edwin's old ID card had allowed them access to the building. The bad news was, he and Patricia only had two such cards, and there were three of them. That would make it difficult for them to split up, should the need arise.

But there was still more good news. When Edwin and Patricia had left their cabin to join Harry in the hunt for Jeff and Chipper, they'd brought along other supplies they thought they might need. They included very small tracking devices no larger than coins.

They'd clipped one to the inside of Jeff's pant leg, and a second to the inside of Harry's belt. But when it had come to Chipper, there had been nothing to clip it to. Under his collar would have been the perfect spot, but nothing could be slipped in there.

"Hmm," Edwin had said.

"I have an idea," Jeff had said. "Chipper could swallow it."

Edwin had looked at the dog. "What do you think about that? It's not much bigger than a pill."

No problem. And, of course, you will get it back eventually. What do they call it? Stoop and scoop?

Edwin had smiled and said to Jeff, "I think he's developed more of a sense of humour since we last saw him."

Now that they were in The Institute, Edwin got out his phone and, using a special app, allocated the signal from all three tracking devices.

"We are good to go," he said.

Edwin had been confident the trackers would not be detected when Jeff, Harry and Chipper entered the building, but he had been less sure about John's gun. There were sensors on the doorways that could pick up large metal items. So John had left his firearm in the van.

Edwin whispered to John, "Jeff and Harry are downstairs in the cell. That's where they'll have Emily, too."

"And probably Pepper," Patricia added.

"Right," Edwin said. "I think that's where we go first. We get the kids and Harry and Pepper, then go after Chipper, who, according to this" – he held up his phone to show them – "is in the lab. Which may mean he's back in a cage. That's where they keep the dogs."

"And where they operate on them," Patricia said anxiously.

"I know."

"What about surveillance cameras?" John asked. "We don't exactly look like we belong here."

Patricia looked around the laundry room until her gaze landed on a stack of cleaned and folded lab coats. "We put those on," she said.

"It won't buy us a lot of time, but it should buy us some," Edwin said, reaching for three coats. He tossed one to his wife and another to John.

Patricia said, "And I know where there might be some stun guns. A little way further down this hall."

"If I run into that Daggert guy," John said, raising two fists, "I can just use these."

The three of them slipped out of the laundry room. When they reached the door to a supply room further down the hall, Patricia used her ID card to get in. The metal shelves along the walls and throughout the room were loaded with boxes.

They scanned the boxes, reading labels.

"I'm not finding anything that says stun guns," John said.

"Me neither," Edwin said.

"Wait!" Patricia said. "Here's a box of them and – nuts! There's just one!"

"Give it to John," Edwin said. "He'll know how to handle it better than either of us."

John accepted the stun gun from Patricia.

"Okay, let's find that holding cell," he said.

Patricia went back to the supply room door, inserted her card, and turned the handle.

The door stayed locked.

"Hang on," she said. "It didn't work."

"Try it again," her husband said.

She inserted the card a second time. And again, the door would not open.

"It won't unlock," she said, turning to give the bad news to Edwin and John. "We're trapped."

42

"Amazing," Madam Director said to herself, sitting behind her desk, viewing the feed from various surveillance cameras within The Institute on her computer monitor. She usually kept that feature running at all times, and the images would rotate among the countless cameras around the building.

"Absolutely amazing."

She had been making a few handwritten notes when some movement on the screen caught her eye. Three people were moving quickly down a hall. They'd exited the laundry room, and were now slipping into a supply room.

She played back the last few seconds from one of the cameras, then froze the image at a point where the faces were clearer.

Two men and one woman.

One of the men, and the woman, looked familiar to her.

She magnified the image. And that was when she said, "Amazing."

The Conroys were alive.

Quickly, Madam Director brought up settings for the security system and locked the supply room door, overriding all other clearances.

"I'll deal with you later," she said aloud. There were other matters to address first. She pressed a button on her desk and said, "Send in Timothy."

Seconds later, the door opened and the six-year-old boy entered.

"Yes, Madam Director?" he said.

She stood up and smiled. "I have a very special job for you."

* * *

Madam Director, Timothy and Daggert stood by the holding cell door.

"Let me explain the situation to you," Madam Director said to the boy. "There is a dog in that room. She looks ordinary, but there's a chance she's a dog with very special abilities. We don't know for sure."

Timothy nodded. "Okay."

Daggert said, "I don't like this."

Madam Director looked at him sharply. "When I want your opinion, Daggert, I shall ask for it. Now, Timothy, we can't employ our usual methods to determine if this dog is special. X-rays, that kind of thing, can't be used. But with your very sensitive hearing, I believe that as you get closer to the dog, you will be able to hear any mechanisms that might be

239

built into her. And if you do, you can tell me about them."

"This sounds easy," Timothy said eagerly.

"Okay then."

"Will you be coming in with me?" the boy asked her.

"Uh, no," Madam Director said. "Daggert and I are going to stay out here in the hall."

Timothy frowned. "Will the prisoners in there hurt me?"

He knew there were three people in the room, in addition to the dog.

"Of course not," Madam Director. "Why would they hurt you? You're just a little boy!"

He nodded confidently.

"I'm ready," he said.

She turned and looked at Daggert. "The door, please?"

For several seconds, Daggert did not move. Then, slowly, he reached up and touched the pad to open the door.

It slid back into the wall.

Inside, Jeff, Harry, Emily and Pepper were clustered in the far corner. They eyed Timothy warily.

"He's one of them," Jeff whispered to the others.

"Yeah, we've met," Emily said.

Timothy smiled. "Hi, everyone." He trained his eyes on the dog. "Hey there, Pepper. How ya doin'?"

The door slid shut behind him.

"You need to be careful!" Emily warned. "You get much closer and something really bad could happen!"

On the other side of the door, Daggert, fists clenched, said to Madam Director, "Call him back."

"I think," she said, "for our own safety, we should move away from this door. Just in case."

She started moving quickly down the hall, but Daggert hung back.

If Timothy can hear just about anything, Daggert thought, *maybe he will hear this*.

"Timothy," he whispered at the door, "it's Daggert. Don't go near the dog. You could get killed. It could blow up."

Thirty feet up the hall, Madam Director stopped and turned. "Come on!"

"If you can hear this," he continued to whisper, "stop and back away. Come back out. Timothy . . . there's something you need to know. I did some checking and—"

"What are you saying?" Madam Director shouted. "What are you telling him?"

Daggert ignored her. "I did some checking and . . . it turns out you're my son. Timothy, are you hearing this? What The Institute did to you, it's not right. I can turn you back into what you were. I can hook you up, make a few adjustments—"

"Stop talking!" Madam Director said.

241

"Come back, Timothy. I swear it's true. I'm your dad."

Daggert decided he couldn't stand there with the door closed one more second. He slapped his hand on the button and the door slid open.

Timothy stood right there, looking up at him.

"Seriously?" he said.

Madam Director was running back. "Daggert! Daggert!"

Daggert scooped Timothy into his arms and shouted at her, "You knew! How could you? How could you do this to my son?"

The cell door was still open.

Inside, Harry whispered, "I think we may have an opportunity here."

Outside, Madam Director blurted, "I don't owe you an explanation."

Daggert shot back, "And I don't owe you my loyalty."

He charged past Madam Director, knocking her in the shoulder hard when she attempted to block his way. She stumbled back, hit the wall, and slid to the floor. As Daggert fled down the hallway with Timothy slung over his shoulder, she screamed after him, "Stop! You'll never—"

She was cut off mid-threat by Jeff.

As he and Harry and Emily and Pepper charged out of the cell and into the hallway, it was Jeff who noticed the security card hanging on an elastic strap around Madam Director's neck. He knew that if they were to have any hope of moving through The Institute, he'd need it.

He reached down, grabbed the card, and pulled as hard as he could. The strap gave way.

"Hey!" Madam Director shrieked.

At the far end of the hall, Daggert opened a door and, a second later, disappeared with Timothy. The three escapees and Pepper were through the same door once Jeff had inserted the card to open it.

Madam Director struggled to her feet, one of her shoes' three-inch heels breaking off in the process. Lopsided, she kicked off both shoes and ran for the door, but once there, she had no way to open it.

She banged on it with both fists. "Open this door!" she screamed. "Open this door or I'll kill you all!"

43

"We have to get that door open," Edwin said.

John, stun gun in hand, looked up at the ceiling.

"Sprinklers," he said, pointing. "If we can get them to turn on, I bet that door will open... Or, failing that, someone will come and open it for us. All we have to do is start a fire."

"I don't have a lighter," Patricia said. "We don't smoke."

"Me neither," John said. He looked at the stun gun. "Find me some crumpled paper."

Many of the boxes in the storage room were filled with files. Patricia dug out some sheets, crumpled them into balls and dropped them on the floor.

"This gun emits an electrical charge," John said. "It might be enough to ignite the paper."

He knelt down, shoved the gun into the ball of paper, and pulled the trigger. The gun went *Zzzzzzkkkk!* and seconds later the paper started to smoke. He picked up the crumpled ball before it was fully engulfed and held it just inches under the sprinkler.

Water suddenly sprayed down from the ceiling. John dropped the flaming ball of paper and stamped it out with his foot. A fire alarm began ringing.

Patricia tried the door.

"It's open!"

She swung it wide and the three of them burst out into the hallway. They heard footsteps coming from the left and turned.

Jeff, Harry and Emily were running straight for them, Pepper trailing them.

"Dad!" Emily cried.

"Emily!" John shouted.

She leapt into the big man's arms so hard she nearly knocked him over.

"I was so scared!" he said.

"You still should be," Edwin said over the ringing of the fire alarm, trying to cut the reunion celebration short. "We haven't gotten out of here yet!"

Harry said, "We head out the back and get in the van! The keys were in it when they brought us in!"

"We can't go yet!" Jeff said. "I have to get Chipper! They're going to cut him open! Where's the lab?"

Edwin said, "Down that hall and to the left. I'll come with you!"

"No!" Jeff said. "You have to save the kids!"

"Kids?" Patricia said.

Jeff told them about the room he'd passed on his way to the holding cell. Edwin and Patricia held each

245

other's eyes briefly. Trying to save children from The Institute's plans was what had started all this in the first place.

"Get those kids out of here," Patricia said to Edwin and the others. "I'll go with Jeff."

"I have a card!" Jeff said, waving the one he'd taken from Madam Director.

While the others went off to rescue the children, Jeff and Patricia headed for the lab.

Employees of The Institute were streaming into the halls and making for the exits as the bells continued to ring. No one paid any attention to Jeff and Patricia as they threaded their way through them.

Patricia pointed to a door marked "LAB". Jeff used the security card to open it. Inside, the intense sound of yapping dogs nearly matched that of the fire alarm.

There, with his back to Jeff and Patricia, was Wilkins, hovering over Chipper, scalpel in hand.

Jeff glanced to the right and noticed a fire extinguisher attached to the wall by a bracket. He thought back to his days working at Aunt Flo's fishing camp, and the time a guest had fired up a barbecue under the dry branches of a pine tree. When Jeff had seen the flames licking so close to those pine needles, he'd grabbed an extinguisher and buried that barbecue in foam.

So he knew just what to do now.

As the dogs continued to bark and the alarm wailed, Jeff grabbed the extinguisher and yanked out the pin to allow the trigger to be squeezed.

He said, "Hey, Wilkins, you're doing that all wrong."

Wilkins raised the knife, spun around and whispered something Jeff could not make out, although he thought it was: "What?"

Jeff squeezed the trigger and buried Wilkins' face in flame-smothering foam. The man staggered backwards, hit the side of the operating table, lost his footing and landed on his back on the floor. He lost his grip on the scalpel, which flew across the room. He spluttered foam and tried to wipe it from his eyes.

Jeff gave him another shot from the fire extinguisher while his mother looked on, a smile on her face.

While Wilkins struggled to catch his breath and regain his vision, Jeff checked on Chipper.

"Please be okay, please be okay."

He ran his hands over the dog, looking to see whether Wilkins had already sliced into him.

"How is he?" Patricia asked, as she started throwing open the doors on all the cages. The dogs jumped out one by one and bolted from the room.

"Chipper's okay!" Jeff shouted as the dog stirred. "He's waking up!"

Chipper tried to rise up on his front legs, but could not find the strength.

"It's okay, I got you," Jeff said, as he gently picked him up.

"Everyone goes free today!" Patricia shouted, as the last of the caged dogs were released. "Now, let's get out of here!"

Jeff gave Wilkins one last look and said, "You might want to think about a rabies shot. You're kind of foaming at the mouth."

As he and his mother went back into the hallway, they spotted the rear ends of the released dogs running further into the building, and then a dozen children rushing towards them. Leading the way were Edwin, John, Harry, Emily and Pepper.

"This way!" Edwin shouted, pointing in the direction they were all running. "We're heading out the main door!"

"Okay!" Jeff cried.

The Institute was in a state of total panic. People were running in all directions, some clutching files and laptops and whatever else they could carry that they thought might be important. For all they knew, the building really was on fire.

Jeff and Emily were the first out of the building, followed closely by the grownups and Chipper and Pepper. They gathered on the front lawn of The Institute. It was now dark, but a series of spotlights had come on. Sirens wailed in the distance. A fire truck burst through the metal gate down at the end of the driveway despite the protests of the guard. Half a dozen police cars followed.

"How'd the police know to come?" asked Jeff, incredulously.

"I made some calls," John said, smiling.

* * *

Back inside the building, Wilkins struggled to his feet. He went over to a sink to rinse the foam from his eyes.

Chipper was gone. All the dogs were gone.

The fire alarm continued to ring.

He half staggered into the hallway. It was empty now. Everyone had fled the building.

Except for one.

Rounding the corner at the end of the hall was Madam Director. Shoeless, her hair off in all directions, lipstick smeared, her eyes filled with fury, she ran stumbling towards Wilkins.

Suddenly, coming around the other corner, were all the dogs that had been released from the lab. They'd made the mistake of running further into The Institute, instead of towards the exit, and were now undergoing a course correction.

The pack was heading for the outdoors, and Madam Director was in their path.

Were it not for the fire alarm she might have heard them stampeding up behind her. But Wilkins could see them and he was in a position to shout out a warning to her.

Well, he would have been, if she hadn't forced him to drink that scalding hot coffee as punishment for saying bad things about her.

"Look out!" he croaked.

But he might as well have said nothing.

The dogs pounced on her as they raced down the hall, bringing her down like a pack of wolves on a lamb.

Madam Director went down, her head striking the marble floor hard. The dogs kept moving, but Madam Director did not.

Wilkins decided to leave her where she was and follow the dogs.

* * *

With all those fire alarms ringing, and sirens wailing, no one even heard the helicopter at the back of The Institute come to life. No one felt the breeze from the rapidly rotating blades, nor did anyone hear it lift off the ground. Nobody saw the man piloting the craft, or the six-year-old boy buckled into the seat next to him.

And it was only the boy who heard the man say, "We are going to find a way to turn you back to the way you were. And we are never coming back here again."

ONE WEEK LATER

44

It was nine in the morning, the sun was up, and Jeff and his parents were sitting on the porch of the isolated cabin Edwin and Patricia had lived in for most of the past year. They were watching Chipper and Pepper running about, playing together, in the yard between the cabin and the forest.

Jeff's parents had used this place to hide out, but they were hiding no longer, and had gone back to using their real names.

Best of all, they were a family again.

They didn't plan on living in the cabin permanently, but it was a good base for them while they decided on their next step. Jeff had said he'd like to move back into their old neighbourhood, which would mean he could go back to the school he used to attend.

Edwin and Patricia thought that was a good idea.

While the last seven days had been wild for them, the rest of the world knew very little of what had gone on at The Institute.

There had been a brief item on TV about a fire at a research centre, but very few details. When the police and fire department first arrived, Jeff and his parents quickly filled them in on what had been going on inside. While there was no fire, there were plenty of other things they needed to know about. Filling in the authorities went a long way to explaining all the dogs running free, and the dozen children without parents wandering the grounds. Child welfare agencies and the local humane society were brought in. The dogs were rounded up, and the children taken away and cared for. Emily cautioned them that if they found a dog that answered to the name Barbara, they'd better not let her lick anyone's face.

But within the hour, a very different set of authorities arrived: men and women in black business clothes like Daggert had worn, with tiny phones tucked into their ears. Jeff watched as they took aside the police officers and fire department officials for long chats.

Eventually, one of them came over to talk to Jeff and his family, as well as Harry and the Winslows.

She spoke to them briefly, keeping to the point.

"This place is shutting down. It's over. No more tinkering with kids or dogs. Anything that's been done to the children or animals that just escaped from this place will be undone. All we want—"

Jeff interrupted. "What's going to happen to Daggert and Madam Director, and will the guy who was going to cut up Chipper be arrested and—"

"I'm talking, kid," the woman said.

"Yeah, but, at least tell us you got those three. And what about Timothy? He said something, just before Daggert grabbed him, that made it sound like he thought Daggert was his dad. Is that, like, possible? And what about—"

The woman made a sideways slicing gesture to cut him off. "Any information we might have on that is classified. I can tell you we did get a man named Wilkins. But Daggert and the boy and Madam Director . . . leave that with us. As I was saying, all we want from you is to return home and never speak of this again. *Any* of it. In return, you'll be left alone. You'll never hear from us, or anyone from this place, again."

Jeff wasn't happy with the deal at all. "Yeah, but—"

His mother put a hand on his shoulder and said to the woman, "Okay. That's a deal."

So Emily went back to Shady Acres with her dad, and Harry Green surprised everyone when he said he was going to return to Flo's Cabins and do some fishing.

"Turns out I like it there," he said to Jeff. "I might even offer your aunt my services, now that she doesn't have you around to help out." He grinned at Edwin and Patricia. "Or, at least until you need me for some *new* mission."

"That will *not* be happening," Edwin said. "But we will stay in touch."

255

Before they left The Institute, Jeff went back in and found in a garbage can the phone he'd been using to talk to Chipper. He redid the settings so the device could actually be used, once again, to make calls. His first was to his friend Kevin, to let him know that they had found Pepper, and that she was okay.

"When are you bringing her home?" Kevin asked.

When Jeff did not answer right away, Kevin sensed what he must be thinking, and said, his voice trembling with emotion, "Why don't you look after her for a while? After all, she's really your dog. And if you move back here, can she come and visit me?"

Jeff promised that she could.

Chipper and Pepper had become instant friends. Pepper completely brought out the natural dog instincts that Chipper's digital intrusions had struggled to hold back. Here at the cabin, a week later, it was fun to watch them playing in the yard, chasing each other, fighting over a stick, racing into the woods to pursue a squirrel.

"He's having such a good time," Jeff said. He looked at his phone to read a message from Chipper. "He says this is the most fun he's had since he lived at the farm, before The Institute took him away."

Patricia was sitting next to her son with a small computer in her lap and a slender cable wound around one hand. "Do you think he's changed his mind, then?" she said.

Jeff replied, "I asked him just before he went outside."

"What did he say?"

Jeff held up his phone so she could read the message for herself.

I just want to be a dog.

Patricia smiled sadly. "And you want to grant him his wish?"

Jeff hesitated. "Not really. But it's not about me. It's about Chipper. It's about what he wants. I made him a promise."

Edwin said, "I'm proud of you."

Jeff shook his head, not wanting to hear it. "I think maybe it's time," he said bravely. "The more I put it off, the worse I'll feel."

His parents nodded their understanding. Jeff got out of his chair, cupped his hands around his mouth, and shouted, "Chipper!"

Chipper and Pepper were engaged in a tug-of-war over a stick. But when he heard his name, Chipper let go, causing Pepper to topple backwards. He raised his head and looked towards the cabin.

Yes?

Jeff was already choking up a little, so instead of replying he waved the dog in. Chipper ran to the cabin and leapt right up two steps to land on the porch. When he saw Patricia with the laptop and the cable, he knew what was up. He looked at Jeff.

I am ready. Are you ready?

"I guess so," Jeff said.

Chipper sat down as Patricia ran the cable from the computer to the port in his collar. She did a few keystrokes and then said, "So what will happen, Chipper, is you really will go back to being a dog. No two-way conversations. You'll understand some words, of course, just like all dogs do. Your name, plenty of commands. But that's all."

Jeff struggled to ask a question. "Will he remember me?"

"Of course," his mother said. "He'll remember all of us. It's just . . . the memories will be less complex. Do you understand all that, Chipper?"

I do.

"And you'll still be able to see. Your eyes aren't real, but I've set things up in your programming in such a way that they'll still work. But no more sonic booms will be coming out of that mouth of yours." She grinned.

That is okay. It always made my own ears hurt when I did it.

"We're good to go," Patricia said, glancing at the screen and then at Jeff. "All I have to do is click here and it's done."

Jeff said, "Let me do it."

He sat down, pulled his chair closer to his mother's, and took the laptop from her.

258

Chipper came closer, resting his snout on Jeff's knee.

Jeff still had the phone in his left hand as he held his right index finger over the computer's mouse pad.

"We're still going to be the best friends in the world," Jeff said. "It'll just be different."

I know. We can do lots of things together. With Pepper. I really like Pepper, even though she is not very smart. But soon I will not be any smarter.

Jeff sniffed. "Yeah. I'll have two dumb dogs instead of just one."

Maybe I should be insulted but I am not.

Jeff had just one thing left to say before he clicked.

"I love you," Jeff said.

I love you, too. I always will.

Jeff clicked.

Chipper continued to rest his head on Jeff's knee for another couple of seconds. He looked up into the boy's eyes, then out into the yard, where Pepper was running around furiously in a circle, as if trying to catch her own tail.

Jeff looked at the screen on his phone.

There was nothing there.

"Chipper?" he said. "Did it work?"

The screen remained blank. Jeff had his answer.

He said, "Go on, boy! Go see Pepper!"

Chipper turned, jumped off the porch and joined Pepper as she continued to run around crazily.

Jeff handed the laptop back to his mom and stood. His parents prepared themselves to take him into their arms, but he stood firm.

"I'm gonna throw the stick around for them," Jeff said, and walked out into the yard.

He was sad, no question about it. But Jeff took some comfort in the fact that Chipper clearly was not.

Chipper had no idea that there was even anything to be sad about. He had never been so happy in all his life.

ACKNOWLEDGEMENTS

Many thanks to everyone at Orion Children's Books, especially Lena McCauley, Thy Bui and Lucy Upton, and at Penguin Random House Canada, Lynne Missen, Kristin Cochrane, Brad Martin and Ashley Dunn. I also want to thank Sarah Heller of the Helen Heller Agency.

Special shout-outs to all the readers, young and some not quite so young, who picked up Chipper's and Jeff's first adventure, *Chase*, and the booksellers and librarians who have helped introduce me to a new audience. You rock.

HAVE YOU READ...?

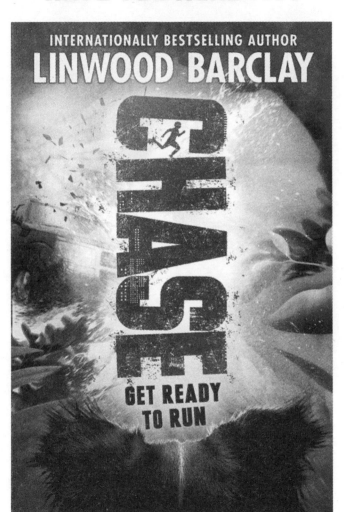

INTERNATIONALLY BESTSELLING AUTHOR
LINWOOD BARCLAY

CHASE

GET READY
TO RUN